IMAGINE THERE'S NO

A Novel

JAMES KEMPER

PAGE PUBLISHING
Conneaut Lake, PA

First originally published by Page Publishing 2022

ISBN 979-8-88654-300-1 (pbk)
ISBN 979-8-88654-301-8 (digital)

Printed in the United States of America

CHAPTER 1

Empty

Is that a dog in the middle of the street? It is, right next to the tubes. Is he lost? A faint wisp rapidly moves from behind me to beyond me in a short second. Where are the passengers going? Why ask? I know—nowhere really. It looks like a German shepherd, not certain though. Why the hell would someone tape up his eyes? It's a *he*, right? Yep, it's a *he*.

It's electrical tape. Is it new? Is it still being made? I haven't seen electric tape in many decades. I remember the smell of it and pressing my thumbnail against the perfectly rolled circle, spinning it so my nail digs under its crisp beginning. But really, it's the end as it was rolled in the factory.

Seriously? Did some dumbass really tape a fucking tampon. Well, I guess it's not a tampon; it's the pad thing, a big white flat cotton thing, over the dog's eyes with electric tape? Maxi Pad—that's what it's called. The tape goes around the dog's head, then under and over his ears multiple times. I can see why he can't get it off; his paws are wrapped in the same electrical tape. Why would someone do this?

He can sense me. His ears flick up and turn toward me. His teeth show without a growl.

"It's okay, boy… You alright?"

Why am I askin' the dog questions? Nice voice; that's it.

"It's okay, buddy. Yeah, good doggie, good doggie."

I feel like I'm talkin' to a baby. Baby, dog, what's the difference? He doesn't seem too keen on me. His teeth are still showin'. Maybe a treat would help out. Do I have anything? I don't think he wants a cigarette. Shit, I would have been arrested for animal cruelty years ago for that. I suppose I could give the dog a cigarette now. No big deal that someone taped up the dog, but that son of a bitch gave him a fuckin' cancer stick—bastard!

Is this a joke? Is there a camera on me somewhere, like the whole hidden camera show? I can't remember the name of it, but I remember how the people in the show got caught doin' stupid shit, and then some guy would pop outa nowhere and say, "You're on hidden camera something or another."

That kind of thing is long, long past. People wouldn't get that humor today. Well, actually, nobody would get any of too much for at least fifty years now. What's this? He has a patch of fur missing. He's been shaved. Looks like about a foot long by maybe four inches high. Definitely shaved, not clipped. All the way down to the light-gray skin. I never knew what color dog skin was. Do all dogs have the same color of skin? No, no; I had a Maltese. When we shaved her, clipped her or rather had her clipped by a professional, her skin was pink. Anyhow, some asshole tattooed this dog on the shaved section. It's faint; it says, "Fuck U."

Maybe it's not a tattoo. Can't be a tattoo; it's not a thing anymore. It could be an ink pen, but it sure looks like a tattoo, almost like an old one—faded light bluish over the gray skin; it's hard to see. I suppose ink pens are sort of a thing of the past as well. Why did they not complete the word *you*? Why just use the last letter? I suppose it still gets the point across. What's the point though?

Only a couple of feet away from him now—don't bite me, big boy. Nobody's out here. Nobody ever is. I should be used to the quiet, only a quiet whoosh from inside the tube from time to time. Noon should be a time when people are gettin' out to do something. It's a beautiful day—the park is right here, no hell below us, above us only sky. I suppose you would have to look at the sky to understand that. Maybe that's why no one is here, except for this tattooed dog.

Aw…he has a collar with a brass tag on it. I can't wait to call the guy who did this. I suppose it could be a girl, but, well, this just doesn't seem like a girl thing, or does it? It really doesn't seem like a thing *any* person would do really, especially these days. This is just plain fucked up. I can't believe I'm witnessing this. Electrical tape somehow smells like electricity to me.

Don't bite, don't bite…almost there. Why am I creeping in with my hand? He can't see me. "Hey, buddy."

His head jerks quickly to my voice. This time he seems calm, no teeth. "Good boy, goooood boy, goooood boy."

A big white elevated cargo tram flutters through the trees in the far distance. I keep forgetting the interstate is at the bottom of that hill. The tubes and the trams are so quiet.

Should I try petting him? I think I kinda have to. Should I call animal control? Where are my glasses? I'll Joogle it. I imagine there's some kinda animal control or something. What does J do with animals? Put them out of their misery? Wish it would do that for me. Okay, bad idea. "It's alright, buddy. We'll figure something out."

It sure looks like a tattoo. He's soft and gentle. He moves his head and neck into my hand. Will he take off if I remove his eye patch? Or is it *eyes patch* since it's one patch for two eyes?

Someone spent some time puttin' this shit on him. Maybe I'll get the owner information before I take this shit off his head. "Let's see here, buddy. Who's your owner? Can't wait to see what sorta strange did this."

That side's blank. "I'm Funny."

What? I don't get it. There's gotta be a camera on me. What the hell? Is his name "Funny"? Why else would the *F* be capitalized?

CHAPTER 2

Winning and Excellence

She doesn't look too special to me. "Hello, you must be Grace."

"Yeah."

"I'm Dr. Bourne. Come in. Follow me."

She walks through the vestibule, the foyer and into my study.

"Your house is funny."

"Just like my dog's name."

She peers over to me like I'm not human. Chuckling, I point to Funny who's lying comfortably next to the fireplace. Her squint portrays skepticism, not curiosity. Her wrinkled little face just irks me.

She's looking at me like she just ate a spoonful of shit. "I get that look a lot. Have a seat, please."

Her white plastic jumpsuit rubs against the surface of my oversized, brass-tacked, patinaed brown leather armchair and makes an unsettling sound. J is a fucking idiot. This shit, seriously, who fucking makes up this crap? I hope J hasn't stopped the research and design on clothing.

Dumb shit hasn't shown one, one iota of smarts in the clothing category in, I don't know, Christ, not one in at least, at least fifty years. It's too fucking smart; it can't be lazy. There must be some science or something behind it: easy to make, easy to clean, doesn't hold germs, probably a litany of reasons that have nothing to do with looking good and certainly no regard to that awful noise it makes. Wearing plastic, or whatever that shiny material is, it has to be uncomfortable.

I get that they have a netted lining so it's not abrasive to the skin, but it's still just. I don't know. It's unsettling, I guess.

Everything everybody wears is white, gray, or black. Is J color-blind? I suppose that makes sense—everything is black, gray, and white. Did I just stumble onto something? I saw the repairs made to the house that used to be owned by the Rezaks a couple houses down the street. It was vacant at the time and still is, like all the other houses in my neighborhood, but they, or rather J, matched the tone perfectly, but not the color. Nobody lived there to bitch about it, so it just stayed that way. The bots that came to do the painting used gray rather than blue. I think it's still mismatched. I didn't get it, but I think I do now. Good thing my house is white. I thought J just fucked up on the paint match, got there to fix it, and said, "Aw, fuck it!"

That can't be right! J can't be color-blind. Everything in the view is in color, very clear and crisp color, far clearer than what I see out of my own eyes. It's as if J heightens the experience of seeing by adding better and more vibrant color. Definitely not color-blind! Scratch that. Dumb idea.

As I pull out my notepad and a pen, the kid interrupts. "Is that paper? I've seen paper in my memos... I didn't really know it still existed. You're a weird dude."

This kid is certainly on a high horse. "Yeah, yeah, I've heard that before. I'll tell you what, you're what I call a kid. The way I see it is that kids like you…well, they can just keep whatever they think is important to themselves. Let's get something straight here, kiddo. I don't give two shits what you think about my paper, my house, my clothes, any of it. Got it? Ya know what?"

Seemingly unimpressed with my rant, "What?"

"You'll never catch me in a plastic jumpsuit."

She frowns. "You don't like my jumpsuit?"

"I don't. I think it's silly."

Her dangling legs cross at the ankles, and her head drops. "Whatever. You smell. Did you piss your pants?"

I look down. What is she talking about? I stand up to check lower. No. Is she messing with me? Can't be. These kids don't know how to do that.

I can't stand the melodic day-to-day nothing. This is not that. I feel my cheeks rise; I chuckle. "Don't you get thumped when you say shit like that?"

"Nope!"

"Really?"

"Mom thinks my earpieces don't work. I get a new pair of them delivered about every day."

Never heard of that before. Anyhow… "Okay, let's get to business. You know why you're here, right?"

Her head remains down. "Because I have to. Somehow, I was singled out for this. I was told to do it. Mom explained that you're not a bot, but still a doctor. A doctor for the mind, not the body. She didn't say much more, just that I had to come here. Out of control or something."

Does she know that she's singled out? She seems pretty oblivious. "Do you know why you were singled out, Grace?"

Instantly her head flips upward, curls bounce, and the kid arrogantly looks directly into my eye. "Not really. I didn't receive much of an explanation, just that I am displaying behaviors that need to be dealt with…somethin' like that anyway, and Mom said it would help me. I don't really get it though. I don't think I need help. Somethin' about me not gettin' along with others. I don't really care. I mind my own business. Just don't like hangin' out with dumb kids at the coffee shop or stupid play dates. What's the big deal? So, what is it? We just sit here and talk, and somehow that makes things better? Seems like a waste of time. And why do I have to call you 'Dr. Bourne'? Are you a bot? If you are, you must be one that…well, I don't know, you're all wrinkly and ugly."

I cross my legs. "Alright, Grace. Let's get started. First, what is the color of your eyes?"

She looks at me like I'm smokin' dope. "What kinda question is that? Why do you care?"

That got her attention a little. "It's a question people ask to get to know the other person. It's called a pleasantry. Makes us feel kind and nice about each other."

Is she considering the idea or not? She just stares at the ceiling. She might just be looking at a new pair of shoes for all I know.

"Blue. What color are yours?"

A little sassy, but nonetheless an answer…and even better, a question! This is damn early for that. None of these kids care.

"Very good, Grace! Mine are what you see. I don't wear the lenses like everyone else."

She sits up straighter, causing that screeching noise again. I can tell she's focusing in on my eyes. I'm sure she's zoomed in to within millimeters, studying to see if I'm telling the truth. I take off my glasses and open my eyelids to show them bigger. In disbelief she asks, "Why? I don't get it. Are you some sorta mutant?"

I extend my arm with glasses in hand, waving them. "These are my lenses. They are called iGlasses. Well, at least they used to be called that. I'm old and prefer this old technology."

Her finger presses the air between us a few times. She must be changing a setting in her view. She asks, "But your eyes are gray? Just like the lenses. I've never seen gray eyes, ya know, without the lenses. Is that a birth defect? In my memos I saw somethin' called *a circus*, I think. They had freaks in them. Is that what you are?"

Okay, this kid has some spunk; I like it. This is worth a thumbs-up, although she may not recognize the gesture; I don't care. "Good job, Grace! See how this works? You can be interested in something outside of your immediate view."

"Job? Sounds familiar. What's that?"

This stuff slips out all the time. "We'll get to that."

The kid smugly shrugs and becomes entertained with something in the far corner of my study, probably hearing about half of what I'm going to say. "Grace. Over here!"

I snap my fingers. Looking directly into her gaze, I smile. "So, for most kids I do exactly what your mom told you, sort of. I talk to them, and I figure out how to ease their tensions. This time in life for kids your age is a difficult one. It's called puberty. With most kids we talk, and I document their feelings and find a resolution to those feelings that makes them happy or content. I then download the individualized resolution so they can be reminded whenever they feel a little off and need some support. It remains documented for immediate access that can be replayed in any voice and face they want to hear and see."

This is so fucking stupid. In the corner of my glasses, the coin accumulates. What's the point? "Grace, I need you to remove your lenses and earpieces."

Look at that face; she's attentive now. "What?"

"Yes, Grace, you heard me. This is how it works here."

Shaking her head, "Mom said I wouldn't like it at first. She said she saw you when she was fifteen as well. I don't understand. It just doesn't seem fair. I didn't do anything wrong. I just don't like being around the other kids that much—well, really, anyone. I don't get the social time stuff. It just seems really stupid. Do I really have to do this? There's gotta be some way that I can just kinda comply with whatever it is that I'm supposed to do, right?"

I take a deep breath and exhale. "Hmm. I'm not positive, but I think most, if not all, kids your age in your neighborhood come here at your age. It's normal, not really that special. Does that make you feel any better?"

Her lower lip curls. "Why would that make me feel any better? Why does it smell so weird in here anyway?"

"Very well then, Grace. Please take off your lenses and earpieces and place them in the box on the table. Right over there."

"Aaaawwwww!"

Lifting the box, she remarks, "This box is heavy."

"Yes, Grace, it is. It's made of lead."

Complying, her right hand goes to her left eye. Nearing touch, she asks, "Really?"

Isn't it pretty fucking clear? "Suck it up."

Taking off my glasses and earpieces, I place my iGlasses in my box and put on my normal reading glasses.

Grace looks around my study without the lenses and points to my bookshelves. "What are all these things?"

"They are called books. I was told you know how to read, right?"

"Of course, I know how to read, and I know what they are. I just haven't seen any in person. It would be difficult to shop if I couldn't read. Duhhh."

"Not everyone can read, Grace. In fact, I don't believe most people your age can read. I bet you didn't know that. I don't know why, but I do know that most of the teenagers who I consult cannot read. That makes you pretty special to me."

It appears as though she's never considered the thought. I can tell she's struggling without her lenses and earpieces; she has no way to get an answer.

"It's okay, Grace. I'm going to fill you in on many things that you won't find in your view. Some of it will be frustrating. You can ask me questions. Like I was saying, for most kids your age, I listen to them for a few sessions, write a narrative of their feelings, and provide them with soothing words that allow them to find calm. It's called cleansing. I don't call it that, but anyhow..."

"What are you cleaning?"

"I suppose the things that frustrate kids your age, like: Why am I attracted to boys or to girls? Or I think I'm ugly, or this or that isn't fair kind of stuff, like you just said. Not real difficult questions like: What is the meaning of life? That question I would love to talk about, but don't with the kids that come here daily. The main purpose are those feelings that pop up at your age. Feelings that make people your age have racing thoughts. I work with them to understand the precise feeling, work with them to find out what would make them feel better about it, and then document the session. The view, as you call it, takes that information and creates an experience that soothes the youngster, cleans the negative thoughts. For instance, if a girl came here, and she was troubled by thinking she was ugly, I would ask her why until she got to the root of whatever it was that bothered her, like her nose was too big."

As Grace touches her nose, I continue, "Depending on how she reacts to the questions, I can figure out if it's really her nose that she's concerned about. Nine times out of ten, it's something else. I'll pull up images of other kids her age and discuss each kid's specific attributes—big ears, big cheeks, little ears, big lips, double chins, on and on. They've usually already done this themselves, but they need someone to kind of get them over the hump that it might be something else they're really frustrated with. One young girl who's probably four or five years older than you thought she was ugly because her eyes were too far apart. After talking about it for a few sessions, we discovered that what really bothered her is that she liked other girls. You know, like *liked* other girls."

Grace makes a gesture like she threw up in her mouth. "Yes, Grace, some girls like other girls. That's okay. Anyhow, this young woman needed some affirmation that it was okay to feel okay about liking other girls since she had not been around too many other girls or women who felt the same way. An experience was created for her that reminded her that it is perfectly natural to feel the way she feels. The view doesn't seem to have the ability to pinpoint what feelings are agitated and what to do about those feelings, so that's where I come in.

"It doesn't seem to be too good at feelings. It's a lot more complex than this, and I don't want, or rather I can't bore you with this. I need your attention. In short, I and my colleagues call it their *mantra therapy*. A mantra is something said over and over that provides a person focus and allows them to escape stress, emotional pain, confusion, and frustration. It's often useful for their entire life. You, you, on the other hand, young lady, for some reason unknown to me, something thinks you should receive something much different. I've been told that you've already received more information than the typical kid and are ready for something entirely different. We'll see though. See how it goes."

"What's that?"

"You'll see."

I roll out my rubber chessboard between us, A1 to my side, and begin placing the pieces. Grace asks, "What is this?"

"Chess."

"What is chess?"

"It's a game."

"I like games. I play them a lot. The one I like the most is called *rollerball.* Have you played that one?"

I look up from setting the pieces. "I don't know any of your games, Grace, and I already know I would not like any of them."

She keeps at it. "I bet you'd like it. I get to pick where I'm at, anywhere in the world, and I roll this giant ball around. It makes really cool sounds, and I can make it go fast or slow. Every once in a while, I make it bounce. Doesn't that sound like fun? Just say 'Rollerball,' and it'll pop up. We need to put the lenses back in first."

Still placing pieces, I don't look up at her. "No."

"Huhhh? Seriously? Are you kiddin' me, Dr. Bourne? You think my clothes suck? Well, yours, yours are about as ugly as what they're on."

Placing the last piece, I sit up. "I am not kidding, Grace. I'd rather watch vomit dry than play your stupid fucking game."

She sits back a little. I doubt that anyone has ever spoken to her with authority. Touching the white plastic figure, "This is a pawn, Grace. It can move forward one or two spaces on the first move and only one on the second move. It can capture any of the black pieces on the board by moving diagonally, like this."

Grace interrupts, "People watch vomit dry? You are a strange man, Dr. Bourne."

"Grace, just focus on the board. See how it moves diagonally to capture?"

"Yes…but why would it capture something else?"

I look into Grace's eyes with a fierce seriousness. "To win!"

It's unlikely that she's heard the word *win* before. Stressing it is important so she understands the power behind the word. I keep looking into her eyes. I can see that she understands that I said something profound, but I doubt she knows what to do with it. She's likely not dealt with much profundity in her life so far. That's all about to change.

Grace scooches into her chair, trying to find a more comfortable position. *Skreeetchh!* "Dr. Bourne?"

"Yes."

"Can you explain *win* to me?"

"Of course. First, let's get you a towel."

Her hands, palms up, lift near her shoulders, and her mouth drops open. "What?"

"Your pants' noise is bugging the shit out of me. Right over there on the sofa…grab that blanket, and sit on it."

Her mouth slowly shuts, and her hands drop to her sides. She peers at me every step to the blanket, grabs it, stomps back to the chair, throws it on the cushion and plops herself down.

That was a little dramatic. Fine. "You be you, Grace… Okay, tell me about some of the things you see during your learning sessions."

"Are you talkin' about memos?"

"Yes, *memos*, as you call them. What you are being shown are small glances of the past, not the whole enchilada. You know, the whole thing. It's a way of introducing you to the past just enough so that if you stumble across anything, you're not overly shocked by it. Can you recall any that make you question the past?"

"I don't know. This all seems so weird."

"Think, Grace. Think hard."

"Well, I suppose I don't get any of 'em really."

"Any stick with you? You know, do you think about any of them from time to time?"

"A few, I guess. One that makes me feel a little uncomfortable was this one that was faded or fuzzy. I remember it had no color. I could make out people that didn't look happy, just like someone just made them take off their lenses and earpieces!"

I tilt my head and look at her through the corner of my eye. "Come on, Grace, stay with it. I know you have the ability to pay attention in there somewhere."

"Okay, okay. Let me think… So, I remember these really skinny people all in line in frumpy, dirty outfits. Then they were naked and falling down. After that, they were stacked on top of each other in piles, not moving. Makes me think the past was pretty bad."

J did communicate some graphics that the other kids would never receive and definitely would not be able to deal with, "It was, Grace. That's what we're going to talk about. Now let's talk about surviving. You see, people are born with a desire to survive. A long,

long time ago, people needed to fight to survive. And they needed to be the best at whatever it was they needed to do in order to survive. They needed to be excellent at something, meaning they had to be better than other people at whatever it was they had to do to survive in order to live, in order to win. Sometimes that meant killing other people.

"You see, before cities were built, before the tube, and before bots came to our houses dropping off food and clothes, people lived in the woods—ya know, in the forests without houses. There was only so much available to them to eat and drink so only the ones who could excel at a craft would survive. Only the ones strong enough or smart enough would get the food. The others would die. It may not be that apparent, but we would die if we didn't eat and drink. Living was directly tied to excelling. People were born with different sizes and shapes. They couldn't help that. What they could help is how well they could do something.

"My point is that we are all born with the ability to learn something and become good, then be great at it. At least most are anyway. The urge to want, that's out of our control. It's deeply rooted in our beings. It's who we are. It's what allows us to excel at things. It's what drove your great-great-great-great-grandparents to live—and the same for the other people you see day to day. Their great-great-great-great-grandparents did the same thing. That feeling, that urge is also what led people to do the terrible things that you saw in your view. It's what you're feeling when you get frustrated, and for most patients, I provide a calm for them. That's what I do. For you, no. Quite the opposite. So…let's play chess. It will help you understand."

CHAPTER 3

The Provider

"I don't understand, Dr. Bourne. I tried to find chess in the view, and I heard the bad thump in my ear and my coin went down."

Did I not tell her? Maybe I didn't. Probably better she figures some of it out on her own. "Let's sit down, Grace. We'll get to that."

"Okay, I guess. How old are you anyway?"

I'm sure she's never seen anybody as old as me. I haven't seen too many as old as me. "I'm a hundred and twenty-four."

"Wow! That's pretty old! I thought Mom was old. She's thirty-five, I think. That must be why you wear those funny clothes and live in this funny house. How old is this house anyway?"

"It's even older than me, Grace. It was built in 1904, and I was born in 1969. Take your lenses and earpieces out, okay?"

I have her box opened for her. She sets them inside and closes the lid.

"Grace?"

"Yeah?"

"You can't talk about chess unless you remove your lenses and earpieces, alright?"

"Why?"

"We'll get to that. Just don't talk about what we talk about here outside of this house. Got it?"

"Yeah, I got it."

"Do you remember how to set up the board?"

"I do."

"Okay then. What are you waiting for? While you set up the board, I'm going to turn on some music. Do you like music, Grace?"

"Yes! Does this mean I can put my earpieces in?"

"No. It does not. This is what's called a record player. It plays music. It plays music that was actually created by people, like you and me. It's not that crap you listen to. That's just a bunch of sounds pasted together by a computer."

Grace frowns. "Do you like anything that I like? What's a computer?"

What do I tell her? "No to your first question, and for the second, we'll get to that."

Let's see here... Beethoven, Brahms, Johnny Cash, Frank Sinatra. Here we go... Mozart. Why not start here, the "Requiem Mass." Let's see how she takes this in.

She's wearing another plastic jumpsuit. I cannot stand the sound of that fucking thing against my chair. It reminds me of when all sorts of things used to bug the shit out of me. Somehow I miss that.

"Put the blanket down, Grace. Ever heard anything like this before?"

She grabs the blanket and throws it on the chair. "No. It doesn't sound like somethin' I would think anyone would listen to on purpose."

At least she's listening. How do I get to this? Oh, maybe this will work. I'll give it a shot.

"How do you get your hair cut, Grace?"

She focuses on the chess pieces. "Mom and I go to the spa every Tuesday."

I have not been to the spa in many years. It just seemed so foreign to me. It was very relaxing, but it was uncomfortable at the same time, lying down in this contraption that looks like an old tanning bed, then trusting that it worked properly. I hear that it does everything now: bath, massage, nails, hair, everything while being entertained. I know that I'd like it, but it just doesn't feel right.

"Is blonde your real hair color?"

"Yes."

"Is it naturally curly?"

"Yes. This music…it's really strange."

"How so, Grace? How does it make you feel?"

"Uncomfortable."

Good, this is working. "How do you mean, Grace? Explain a situation that made you feel uncomfortable like this music makes you feel."

Her mouth opens in a sarcastic gesture. "You sure ask a lot of stuff that just seems weird."

"Just answer my question, Grace."

"Uncomfortable, uncomfortable, let me see… Oh, okay, yeah, I think somethin' like… My friend Micha had a dog, a small one, not big like Funny. One day it was just gone. She said she was told that it ran away. I liked the dog. It was white and fluffy and jumped around. I didn't believe her at first—that it was gone, ya know. I looked around her house, and Whitey wasn't there. That made me feel, I don't know, just kind of not right, I guess. I suppose this music is kinda like that."

Mozart may really touch the essence of humanity. That's not what I was going after, but this is good. "Okay then, back to your hair. Do you care about the way you look?"

Grace's head jerks from the board. "What are you talkin' about? Of course, I do. Doesn't everyone?"

"Most people do, I think. Not as much as people used to, but yes. People, well, women used to wear makeup to make themselves look better. I always thought it was a little silly. Anyhow, what I want to know, Grace, is why. Why do you care?"

Grace squints at me like I made a silly face. I repeat, "I'm serious, Grace. Why?"

Her squint remains, but she seems more thoughtful. "I'm not sure, Dr. Bourne. I guess I don't want to be ugly like some of the other kids who come to you and think that about themselves. I don't think I am ugly. I guess I like it when I see boys look at me—not like they ever say anything, or even if they did, nothin' would happen. They probably get thumped and move on. I guess that makes me feel okay."

I look at my old, worn hands. "Well, Grace, not everyone feels good about themselves. You didn't like that I don't like your stupid jumpsuit, right?"

"It's not that I didn't like that you didn't like it. I don't care what you think."

She said that with the utmost confidence.

That piece is in the wrong location. "Grace, you have the bishop and the knight switched around."

"Oh! Sorry, Dr. Bourne. Here we go."

That's better. "Alright. I'm moving my king's pawn forward two. The reason I'm doing this is to give myself the ability to move my bishop and queen, while at the same time protecting these two spaces. This space here, Grace…"

As I point to the space she replies, "Yep."

"This space is critical. If I can get a knight in this space, it will be protected. See that?"

"I think so. Tell me more about winning. I think I'm sorta gettin' the gist of it, but I'm not really sure."

"Very good then. Going back to survival. In order to survive, we had to become really good at something. That's engrained into the fabric of who we are. Inside our brains, we are wired to want to do what is necessary to survive. And that used to mean, I think that's accurate, used to mean that we needed to excel at something. So you see, it's really a *something* of the past, but not really. As we've discussed, we have it in our DNA somehow, the *want* to survive, keep going, keep our kind alive, passed down from parent to child, parent to child, and so on, and it's not something we can just get rid of, so we act on it. You act on it without knowing it. It's a thing that we need to understand before we can work on it. It's an impulse, Grace. It's not your fault. It's really not a fault, but for most, it's my job to strip that *want* from them. It gets in their way of having a happy life somehow. Excellence and winning are not for everyone, Grace."

Grace moves her king's pawn as well. "I'm not mocking your move, Dr. Bourne. Even though I couldn't play since our last session, I've thought about it, a lot and this opening move seems to make sense. It allows the queen and the bishop to move. I still don't really get the whole winning thing."

She is really curious. Maybe J's right. What is it usually? Three maybe even five sessions before any of these dumbed-down kids can partially fathom that they are born with an urge. She got that right away. I would never talk to them about real-life stuff like winning.

"It's a good move, Grace. I didn't think you were mocking me. So, when you win, it means that someone else has lost. What's important is that you understand that when you excel at something, someone else might lose. That's why I'm asking if you feel good about the way you look. You see, if you can get the attention of a boy, like you mentioned, over some other girl…you know, the boy looks at you versus the other girl, well, you have won, and the other girl has lost. Get it? It's very subtle, but it does exist. What I'm going to teach you about winning is on a far different level than catching a boy's attention though. I'm going to share with you how it used to be. It's good to know where we came from so we can learn from it. Your slate is clean. It might be a little traumatic to get into all of it too quickly, so we'll ease into it."

She was about to touch her knight. She stops her hand just above the mane of the knight. Frozen, she slowly raises her head. "Are you messin' with me, Dr. Bourne?"

"I'm not, Grace. The want to win at something is alive. I think you are getting a small glimpse of it. It can be ugly. The saying goes 'Alive and well,' but I'm not sure about the well part all the time. What's missing in most people today is recognizing that it exists and why it exists. They simply feel the urge that we've been talking about and don't know what to do with it. It confuses them, and they become frustrated. It remains that way until they find something to do with it. You know the streets around here that don't have the tubes?"

"I know they exist, but I'm told they're off-limits."

"They are to you, Grace. The few people there are not bad people—or good people. They are people just like you and me, but they have not been taught how to deal with their anxieties, or as I've been telling you, their urge. There aren't enough people out there like me trained to provide support, so they don't get the mantra therapy like your mother did. Without it they act out—nothing too bad, usually just dumb pranks, which they are kind of punished for—thumps, fuzzy views, the loss of coin—but they never quite find the peace of mind that can be gained through some good old mantra therapy."

Grace moves her knight. "Mom calls me spoiled. She says that I'm lucky and I don't know it. Is that what she's talkin' about?"

I nod my head. "Sort of."

I point to Funny. "You know Funny?"

"Yeah, so what?"

"I'm pretty sure Funny came from the people who don't have access to anxiety control, the people who live where the tubes don't go. I think they abused him."

Grace looks at me like I spoke in Chinese. "Huh?"

How do I address this? I guess I brought it up, but I'm not going to go too far; not sure it fits into the purpose here.

"They have the exact same conditions we have. They are sent food, clothes, lenses, all that. They have their own coffee shops and ice cream parlors, but what they don't receive is personalized therapy. Their frustrations are not helped, not calm, so they act out like I was saying. Anyhow, I found Funny by the tube out front here. He had stuff taped around his head, and a part of his side was shaved. Really not that bad or anything, just dumb as hell. I call it abuse because it was. Overall, Funny is just fine and better off here, but it's an example of what people do when they don't know what to do with their urge. People call it all sorts of stuff—dominance, sex, power, all sorts of things. I like things simple, so I just lump it in one big category: to win, whatever form winning means to them."

Grace looks at me like I'm losing her. I need to get back on track here. "Stick with me, Grace. I'm going to switch gears slightly. Let me put a different record on for this. I'm moving my knight, here… Think about your next move while I change the record."

This should do the trick. "This is Wagner, Grace. It's called 'Flight of the Valkyries.' So where were we? Oh, yeah, let me show you something."

Here we go. "See this?"

I flip my laptop open and press the power button. "This is a very old computer, Grace."

She doesn't seem too impressed. I open up my latest book and show her the screen. "This part right here, it's called a keyboard. This is how people used to type to write books. That's what I use it for now. It could be used for many different functions such as accounting, and…"

She's not going to understand any of this. "Anyhow, so the view is created by a computer. I think you asked about computers the other day when I let the word slip out. A computer is a man-made thing. Made a long, long time ago to help us do the things we didn't want to do, like math or finding stuff in an encyclopedia. I know, Grace, I know. I see your confusion. Let me think here… I'm not used to talking about this stuff. Give me a second… Okay, okay, let me start over. A computer is a thing, not a human. A computer stores information and processes it. Not unlike a human brain, but it operates without emotion. It doesn't have the urge to want. It doesn't have a desire to win. It just takes the information it has and spits it back out. That's what your view is. It's a computer. Got it?"

Grace looks at my laptop, back at me, and shakes her head. "I don't think so. I moved, see?"

"Perfect, thank you. Alright, so what's important is that computers, the view, all of it, it's not human like us. You see, it doesn't get everything we're about although it kind of runs us. The whole thing I've been saying about how it can't do what I do…hold on."

"What are you sayin', Dr. Bourne? I'm really confused now."

Grace will like this move. I move my bishop to protect my knight's next move. Okay, good. Where was I? Oh, yeah.

"So, Grace, most people don't live as old as me. I really shouldn't be alive. I've had two liver transplants, new knees, heart surgeries, and all sorts of injections that keep me going. I even got a new asshole so I don't shit myself. I actually look a lot younger than I really am. I look more like a seventy-year-old, although you wouldn't know that."

Grace still looks baffled. I add, "You see, I drink a lot. I drink like a fish and smoke like a chimney. I should be dead. Have you seen smoking in your memos?"

"Yeah, but never in person."

"Well, it's not good for you and doesn't really exist anymore. Anyhow, where I was going was that whatever it is that takes care of us, provides the view…you know, the computer…well, it somehow knows this and gets me to the hospital when I need it. It tells me what it's doing, fixes me, and brings me home. It sends a nurse bot to comfort me and gets me the shit I need. It doesn't do this for everyone. The average life span now as I and my colleagues figure is actually less than half my age—somewhere around fifty-five."

Grace looks like she's seen a ghost. "We can talk about this? The provider? Can you talk to it?"

I suppose that's a good way of explaining J: "the provider." I smile. "Just as long as our lenses and earpieces are in the box, and, yes, I talk to it, sort of. More like it talks to me."

Her attention doesn't fade—my opportunity to really dive a little deeper.

"So, check this out. I often walk through those neighborhoods we were talking about. I don't see anyone under the age of thirty-five, your mother's age. The way I figure it, they can't have kids. I'm sure you've noticed that there is nobody between the ages of twenty and thirty in your neighborhood, right? I can guarantee you, Grace, there isn't. Nobody! Have you noticed?"

Grace tilts her head. "Not really, no."

I continue and speak very clearly, enunciating every syllable clearly. "Nobody exists between the ages of twenty and thirty. Nobody exists between the ages of two and twelve. And in the neighborhoods without the tubes, nobody exists under the age of thirty-five."

Grace says nothing, just looks with something between disbelief and amazement. I point to the board. "Your move, Grace."

She's hooked. She looks at her gray shiny jumpsuit that is plastered to her thin frame, touches her head, and slides her fingers through her hair. She opens her mouth and says nothing.

"You're what's called *lucky*, Grace, like your mom said, and so am I. I'd bet the ranch that nobody, especially those in the neighborhoods without the tubes, would ever receive the medical care that I do. 'Bet the ranch' is an old saying. It means I'd risk all my coin that what I'm saying is correct."

Grace frowns. "I've thought about what sends us stuff every day. I've tried asking Mom about it, but she turns her head, my ears thump, and I lose coin. Can I really talk about it? Here? Right now?"

I look around and pretend like someone's watching us, smile, and whisper, "You sure fucking can."

Her eyes become gigantic, speechless. I add, "That's the whole point of you being here, Grace, to talk about the things you can't talk about every day with your lenses in. You see, the pieces on this board are kind of like people. People are different, and they can do different things. They are like people who you have control of. Ultimately you use them, and let some of them die so that others can live. There's an old saying: 'Every man for himself.' Does that make sense, Grace? The saying?"

"Yeah, I get it."

"Good, so the game teaches us that it's not about the strength of each person, but rather the strength of everyone working together as a whole to excel. It really doesn't have to be that someone else loses, but in our past, well that's really what happened. Just like this chess game. In order to make something better, you've got to understand what that something is first. So, we play chess, Grace. We learn what is in our nature, then we step back. We discover that which we are, that which we didn't know about ourselves, then we can move forward."

CHAPTER 4

Woodsmen and Beans

"Does your mom ask about our sessions?"

"She doesn't. Not a word. We just go about like nothin' is happenin'. It didn't seem weird at all before, but now… Now it just seems really weird!"

"That's okay, Grace. It will become normal. Trust me. We've got a lot more ground to cover, but soon, you'll understand. Trust me."

Grace studies the board in front of us that we didn't finish the last session. Even though I've been explaining that she should drop her king, she insists that she can figure a way out of the inevitable checkmate.

I interrupt her deep thought. "Do you want to win, Grace?"

Still looking at the board, she replies, "I don't know. What cuts your hair?"

Is she being clever? I don't know that I've been asked this before. Is this humor coming from a kid? I laugh without trying. "I cut my own hair, Grace."

She looks at me with skepticism. "Must be why you look like that."

My brown corduroy jacket must be fifty years old. The ridges are worn smooth on my inner arms and abdomen. Those areas are a light brown now. My pants are about the same. I used to wash them in the washer and dryer, but for a long time now, they've been picked up and brought back the same day, clean, folded neatly, and sewn up when necessary. They do a really good job. I don't have a Chinese guy or gal to say "Hi" to and shoot the shit with; it just shows up. Look at that, my ring, many sizes too small, my wedding ring. My beautiful wife. God, I love her.

People that die now, they just die. The bots come and take them away. Their families just look on, like they aren't sure what's happening. I'm sure they ask about it and get thumps in their ears until they stop. I knew my wife was dying, and she knew it. Nothing came to heal her like they did for me; I wish they had never come for me. It took two and a half weeks. She suffered, I suffered, we felt. I cried and cried and cried. I buried her in the backyard. God, I love her.

Grace interrupts my thought. "I think you were right."

What is she talking about? "About what?"

"The people who don't exist. Ya know—ages twenty to thirty. I tried finding some, and my ear thumped, and I lost coin. I tried a couple more times. Finally, my view went all fuzzy. It frightened me."

Another good lesson. Maybe a little harsh. "You need to be careful talking about what we talk about here, alright? Don't mention any of this to anyone, not even your mom. Do you ever have conversations with anyone without your lenses in?"

"No, why would I?"

"Okay, good! Keep it that way. At least for now. I told you that you were special. I'm telling you things I tell very, very few of my patients. Actually, in your case you're not a patient. You're a student. I didn't tell your mom this stuff. I didn't play chess with her. She received the mantra treatment like everyone else and was told about the urges a lot different than the way I've introduced it to you. Got it?"

"I got that. I just don't get it."

Time to feed her a few more scraps. "I understand your confusion, Grace. I really do. Today we're going to talk about the beginning, or at least where I think it may have started. Okay? It will take a while before all the pieces come together. Ready?"

Raising her eyebrows, she looks directly into my eyes, almost sweetly. "Yes, I'm ready."

"Okay, make your move first."

She looks at the board. "I give in." She points to her king. "What do I do here?"

"Drop it, then reset the board. I win. How does that make you feel?"

While she moves the pieces, "Not sure, Dr. Bourne. I guess this means I lost. I don't really feel anything. Maybe I feel like I would rather win. It's a tough game, and for some reason which I don't understand, I sorta want to be good at it. The way it all works, at least as I'm gathering, is that to be good at it, really good at it, well, you need to be better than someone else. Is that right?"

That makes me happy. "You are getting the point. The real point is to be excellent at something. In chess, it means someone else loses, but it isn't always that way."

I look around and really grasp how differently I live than everyone else. I have paintings on the walls from long-forgotten artists. What do these kids think about that? Everly…she asked about them. She couldn't believe that a person created them. I'm not sure she ever will.

"Okay, Grace, where were we? I'm old, and my mind wanders around sometimes."

"The beginning."

"Awww, yes. So, I recall I mentioned that people lived in forests without homes, right?"

"Yes."

I used to sit right over there, next to the fireplace with my beautiful wife. Why am I thinking good thoughts? We fought like cats and dogs at times, but those don't come to mind. Why is that? Her smile is etched in my mind, nothing else. Other shit in the past isn't so beautiful. Why is that? I remember reading about Abraham Lincoln and the struggles he went through. He never agreed with slavery; even as early as a teenager, he wrote about how enslaving someone was wrong, but he didn't really do much about it until late in his first term as president in his midfifties. He had patience, as I deduced from all I read about him. He was also troubled. He had terrible bouts of depression. Ending slavery was a goal of his, but he needed to wait for the right time. That was a lot of waiting, a shit ton of it.

Good—what were good things that happened? Ronald Reagan was a great role model. He fought for respectable ideals. Respectable, yes… Donald Trump was not one of those. He said something about grabbing women's pussies. Although it made me laugh, it also made me cringe. I remember he did some good things, didn't he? Most of my friends thought he was a douchebag. Oh, shit! That's right. My wife voted for him even though he made those statements about grabbing pussies. That is so funny. I miss her.

I suppose I drifted for a second. "Okay, Grace, sorry. Who do you love, Grace?"

Her posture slouches. A frown replaces open eyes. "You ask some stupid questions, Dr. Bourne!"

"Okay then, we'll get back to that one. Anyhow, you probably pictured those people in the wilderness in white plastic jumpsuits, right?"

Grace holds on to a look of bewilderment. "I don't know! Where are you goin' with this, Dr. Bourne?"

I pause and restart. "Okay, so the people in the woods. What do they eat?"

Grace's face changes. She looks to the ceiling for an answer. She looks like she's trying hard and finally blurts, "I don't know."

"Good, Grace, good. Understanding that you don't know something and wanting to know it, well that's what is important as we move ahead. They ate what they could find. Nothing brought them anything. They ate berries and animals. I'm sure you see the little red berries that grow on the shrubs outside my house, right?"

"Yeah."

"Not those exact berries, but they looked around the woods for similar berries and ate them. Don't eat the berries off my shrubs though, Grace. They aren't good for you. They'll make you sick. So, the people in the woods many, many years ago didn't wear plastic pajamas. They wore furs from animals they skinned and had eaten. They wore the skins for clothing not only because they kept them warm when it was cold, but also did it because they somehow felt naked. You eat that white soupy shit every day, right?"

"Soup, yes. Why are you calling it shit? White soup, Diet Coke, and a white brownie. That's what everybody has. I also have a coffee at the coffee shop and sometimes an ice cream at the ice cream shop with Mom when we do our out time. What do you eat?"

White brownie? Isn't a brownie brown? Isn't that why it's called that? Whatever… "I eat much differently than you, Grace."

Raising my tumbler, "This is not watered-down Diet Coke. This is scotch. Scotch is why I've needed two new livers. I know you have no idea what scotch is…the same with cigarettes. Check this out."

I reach in my coat pocket, pull out my package of Marlboro Smooths, open the lid and notice Grace's sense of wonder. She's never seen one. I don't think many people have. I light it up. "This is what I was talking about when I said I smoke."

The cigarette seems to have blown her mind more than anything else that's transpired. I explain, "You see, Grace, I get almost anything I ask for. Even if it doesn't exist around us, somehow it shows up on my front step. I'm pretty damn lucky, or unlucky depending on how you see things. I don't know how they, or it, does it, but hey, I'm here, and I'm going to make the best of it. My old friend had a saying, 'Makin' the best of a bad thing.' He also said, 'Makin' chicken salad outa chicken shit,' but that one takes some explaining, I'm sure."

Grace's mouth is still open. She flinches. "No way!"

I smile. "That's right, Grace."

I don't think the other kids could handle this. "Let's get back to the point here, alright?"

She smiles. "Okay."

"So these people in the woods, they're actually called cavemen, but I don't want to explain that now. They lived in the woods, so let's call them woodsmen for the time. They lived that way for thousands and thousands of years. Nobody knows exactly how long, but specialized testing of their bones indicates about two hundred thousand years. I know you can't do math, but you can count, right?"

Still focused on my cigarette, she slowly answers, "Everybody can count, Dr. Bourne."

"Yeah, that's right. I guess it sort of slipped my mind. I'm old. I miss some pretty basic stuff sometimes. Anyhow, these people adapted to their environments. They learned how to farm crops and raise animals rather than looking for food in the woods and hunting animals."

I can see that I'm losing her to my cigarette. She probably has little to no idea what crops are or what hunting is. I bend over slightly. "Grace?"

"Yeah?"

"Do you know what's in the white stuff you call *soup?*"

"It's just soup, nothing else. Can you put some music on?"

Oh, that's funny. I love it—just soup. "Well, you're way off base on that, kiddo—the soup thing. And, yes, I'll put a record on."

As I laugh on my way to the record player, I look back and see her squinting and shaking her head in disgust. Not sure why, but I don't really care. "Ya see, Grace, that white stuff you eat that you call soup is made from beans. A bean is a vegetable. What you called *the provider*, let's call it *It*, Okay?"

"Sure."

I cannot stand that answer. I made certain my kids understood what that answer communicated. I'm not certain they ever listened though.

"So, It made this huge, worm-looking device, bigger than my house big. The metal worm digs tunnels called mines through the earth and plants seeds that grow into beans which It harvests…you know, digs up and then makes the white soup from them. The beans are white because they are grown underground without natural sunlight. It figured out that a specific type of gas that's phosphorescent, meaning it glows, could provide the light required for the beans to grow.

"When people were still able to, or more accurately, wanted to know what was happening, they studied the mines and shared images, videos, and stories about what they saw. Not long after this news, maybe a year later, people were unable to have kids. That was the first of many reproductive blank periods. People theorized that the gases used in the mines caused sterility. After a few years, when people were able to have kids again, and they still ate the products produced from the beans, most people quit believing that theory. So that's where your white soup comes from, Grace. How do ya like them apples?"

Grace is bent over the front of the large leather chair, elbows on her knees and chin in her hand. "What's a bean look like?"

"Good question, Grace. Let me see if I have a picture. Give me just a second."

Maybe the encyclopedias; that may be difficult to find…no. The dictionary might have a drawing of it next to the definition. Let's see here…grabbing the large book from the seven-foot-high shelf—not so easy anymore. This thing is dusty. "Whooh."

I guess the cleaning bots don't have a tool to get to the top of these things. "There might be an illustration in here, Grace. This is a dictionary. It contains most of the words in the English language. There are many words in here that you've never heard. Here it is. Right here, Grace."

Placing the opened book in her lap, I laugh at her reluctance to touch it. She places her hands on the book awkwardly. I comment, "It's not going to bite you for Christ's sake."

I point to the picture of a bean plant. "See those stringy things hanging off the plant? Those are beans. The beans get chopped up and mixed in with some water to produce your soup."

As I grab the dictionary and walk back to the bookshelf, her eyes follow the book. "There sure are a lot of words in there."

I tap the hard cover. "There are, Grace. All these books have words in them."

She gives me a *no-shit* look. "Is there a drawing of an old creepy, smelly guy next to your description in that book?"

Still pointing to the walls in my study, floor to ceiling with books, I blank out on a reply to that smart-ass comment. Grace jumps in, "Have you read all of them?"

Looking around…not that one, not that one, or that one. "Oh, I guess I've read most of them, Grace, but not all—probably ninety percent."

Still looking around my study, she softly adds, "I've never read a book. It never occurred to me that books really existed. The memos only show them every once in a while and don't really explain what they are. I didn't think they would be that heavy. Will I ever get to read a book, Dr. Bourne?"

"If you excel."

"At chess?"

Well, that's not what I was thinking, but that may not be a bad idea. "That sounds like a terrific idea, Grace. Maybe even earlier than that."

"How do I excel?"

"You try. Really hard. Do you think you can do that?"

She looks at the chessboard. I sit down opposite her in my leather armchair. She looks up at me. "I think I'd like to…try."

What am I thinking? "Grace!"

"Yeah?"

"Let's do a field trip!"

"What's a field trip?"

"That's not important. Follow me."

Why didn't I think of this earlier? It's right here in my backyard. "Over here, Grace."

Pointing through the window in my kitchen to the backyard, "See that?"

"I do. What is it? Weeds?"

"We're going down there."

These steps are getting harder to navigate every day. "Come on, Grace. I think it's ready to pick."

What is this? Maybe a little closer…the green spikey things on this shrub, surround a brown textured ball, like a mini pinecone. Is it a seed? Look at them all! There are thousands of them. They're every-where, covering the shrub head to toe. Wow! There's potential life inside all these seeds. A little living thing burning to become some-thing more inside each little brown cone. And the shrub lives. Look at all this life. Can J monitor something like this? Literally, see it like I'm seeing it? Well, not really seeing, just understanding what I see: the living and the potential living things versus that which is not—my porch, that fence, the garage, my house. Can J see the difference between them? I bet it can. I bet it can see a lot more. I suppose that I've really only created this new frame, or perspective of viewing life this way—I suppose because I'm thinking of what J would see.

I haven't been outside today. It is truly a lovely day. The birds don't mind all this weird stuff going on in the world. They haven't been any different since I was a kid. They just fly around this way and that way with what seems to be no purpose. But they just keep at it. The little ones seem more random than the big ones. The big ones fly in straight lines and don't flap their wings as much. "This tall stuff right here is corn."

"Okay, so what?"

"So what? Well, you can eat it. This is a garden, Grace. People used to plant gardens so they had fresh food. People can still do it. They just don't know they can. It's a lot better than white soup and Diet Coke, believe me."

"It doesn't look like somethin' someone would eat, Dr. Bourne."

"The part you can eat is right here. It's called an ear. It's behind all this. Let me show you."

It's really not quite ready to pick yet; I must have planted them late. It's not far from our first snowfall. I'll show her one anyway; won't hurt anything. "This is called shucking. Shucking the corn. These little white things right here."

"Yeah?"

"That's what you eat—the part you eat. The rest of it you don't. It's not really ready yet, but you can still taste it. Here, like this… You try, just a little though. Your stomach probably isn't used to real food, so we'll take it slow. Just a taste, alright? Don't swallow."

"Okay. It's hard. It makes a sound in my mouth. Is it supposed to do that?"

"That's called crunchy, Grace, and, yes, that's what it does. When it's fully developed, these little pieces become a little bigger, and softer, and turn yellow. Check these out over here. C'mon, you can walk through it. It won't bite."

"It's really tall and kinda itchy."

Pointing at the ground, "This is a real bean plant, Grace. The skinny things coming off the plant, those are beans! Why look through a book when we've got them right here?"

She doesn't seem as fascinated with it as I. Oh, well… "Alright, Grace, that's probably enough for the field trip. Let's go back in."

This doesn't make sense to me; it should be harder to go up steps than to go down them, but it just doesn't work that way… funny. I should probably let him out. "Funny, come here, boy. I've never asked you, Grace. Do you have a dog?"

"We don't. We talked about it a few years ago, but never really finished talking about it. We just sorta… I don't know… I guess we got distracted."

The lives of these people are so unamazing. It's like a big zoo full of tired-looking lions. Lions with big manes and big teeth, but they just sit around, and let the flies scamper around on their faces. The flies don't know they're in a zoo, and they act as if they're in the wild. The lion… I don't know what it knows. It somehow doesn't seem right, but I suppose it's better than not being at all, right? The pioneers…now there was a time when each moment mattered. Life and death were all around. You really had to be on your game to excel back then. I hope I remember to talk about that with Grace: pioneers, pioneers, pioneers. Picture that! A covered wagon strolling into this place. What the hell would they think? What would these people think? Oh my God, that would be a sight! Would they be scared? Do they really know what being scared is?

Grace points at Funny's turd. "Shouldn't we pick that up?"

"Nope. That's called fertilizer, Grace. Funny's business helps the plants grow. Get it? Funny's business?"

Of course, she doesn't. I think she's getting used to not knowing what I'm saying and just lets it go. I signal, "Let's go back in."

Grace seems amused with my backdoor. "It makes a funny noise. What is it?"

"It's called creaking. You probably live in one of those new homes, don't you?"

What am I thinking? Of course, she does. She looks around my kitchen. "Newer than this. What's that?"

Is she pointing to my stove? Yep, she is. "I use that to cook with, Grace. Like I said before, I don't eat the soup. I pick the vegetables from the backyard and cook them right there."

"Sorta like a microwave?"

"Sort of. I've got one of those too. Let's get back to the study."

Grace slides her hand across the burners as we walk by.

"Alright, Grace, where were we?"

"I don't remember…beans?"

Beans? That's right, we were talking about the underground farms. How cavemen ate versus how she eats. "So, the wood people…"

"I thought they were called woodsmen."

"Right. Anyhow, the woodsmen, over time, a lot of time, thousands and thousands of years, they learned things. As I said, they farmed and raised animals to eat. People used to eat animals."

Grace interrupts, "Like Funny?"

That was funny. "Not dogs like Funny, but other kinds of animals. They actually taste really good, Grace. I imagine dogs taste like shit. I haven't eaten animals for a very long time. I don't even know if those kinds of animals exist anymore. I doubt that cows and chickens would fare well in the wild. Let me try that again. I don't think they would excel in the wild. They would likely die without having people take care of them. Come to think of it, Grace, I used to keep a bow and arrows by the backdoor. I may still have it around here somewhere. Anyhow, many years ago I would shoot rabbits and squirrels. They are pretty good to eat. You need some sauce for the squirrels though. They taste shitty without sauce. If I can find that bow and arrows, I can shoot a rabbit for us. Or I could make a trap, and if I can catch a male and female rabbit, I could breed them. I still have chicken cages in the garage. I could keep them there."

Grace rolls her eyes and makes her move. Not a bad move… I continue, "After a while, the people figured out how to work together. Some would make tools. Others would farm animals, and others would make clothes, and so on. They formed small towns that over many, many years would become big cities. Much bigger than the city we live in. How does that make you feel, Grace?"

Grace looks up from the board. "Why do you care? So, let me get this right. Nobody else knows this stuff?"

"Very few, Grace."

She stares at me questioningly. "You're not makin' all this up, are you? I mean, why would you? Why don't other people know? Why don't you tell them as well?"

Finally, real conversations. God, I've missed this. I wonder if she can see the gratitude in my pause.

"This is what people wanted. People wanted all the comforts of life without the work and the worry. This is where we ended up. People quit caring about the past. When these lenses came out, people were already addicted to what were called cell phones. After the blind death virus, nobody really went out much anyway. Everyone could work from home and saw the world through their cell phones. Those who could still see anyway. I'm making a joke… Okay, probably a bad one. Anyhow, restaurants, bars, and things like the coffee shops you go to didn't really exist anymore. They all went out of business. It recreated them to give people something to do, I suppose. So, the cell phones…parents gave them to their kids at a young age, and, well, most of the population was brought up on them and people didn't really want to do anything else. The lenses just sort of put the nail in that coffin.

"There are a lot of other factors in it all, and that will come a little later here. The big picture is that It is holding on to the past by taking care of me and others like me. It has something in mind. We don't know exactly what the plan is. Some think It wants to slowly bring everyone out of their stupor over time but is waiting for the right way, the right answer on how to do it. Maybe introduce excelling, as I call it, back into the mix, but in a good way, a productive way. Others think It wants to hold on to history so that somebody knows. Sort of like a tree falling in a forest, and no one can hear it."

I can tell she's fading. "Never mind, Grace. we'll lead up to all this stuff. I'm saying a bunch of crap you won't entirely understand.

I know that. But it will make sense before too long. For you…keep at it. Use that urge to excel. Keep it alive, and you can be part of whatever it is."

Grace doesn't seem impressed or convinced. I don't think I really convinced myself either. I think she's taking it pretty well, though.

CHAPTER 5

Empathy

Grace walks in the door, pats Funny on the head, and goes to her chair. "Notice anything?"

Her eyes are blue, not gray. Look at that! "You're not wearing your lenses?"

She gives me a "duh" look. "You told me not to."

"Oh, that's right. Just on the trip over here though. Keep them in for the rest of the time for now, alright? Oh, and…" I point to the blanket. "Blanket."

"Okay, okay. You don't have Funny sit on a blanket when he's on the couch."

"He doesn't wear a stupid plastic costume."

Our chessboard is looking pretty good for Grace, at least for her not to get in trouble anytime soon.

"Tell me about your trip over here. Anything special without the lenses?"

"It was boring, like watching puke dry."

She is a little entertaining. I hope she doesn't stop it now. It's refreshing. "Anything, Grace?"

"Not really. Kinda boring, I guess. The mobile I got into had a kid in it, a boy about my age. He looked pretty normal, I guess. He didn't really pay much attention to me…probably paying rollerball."

Is she still stuck on that? "Do you wish you were playing rollerball?"

As she studies the board, "Sort of, I guess."

"Anything else, Grace?"

She is really thinking through her next move. She can take my knight, but if she does, I will take her bishop with my bishop and split her king and rook. I told her about the split. Let's see if she remembers. It must be why she's taking so long here. She looks up at me.

"I asked the boy where he was going. At first, I thought he didn't hear me. He just sat there doin' nothin' at all, just staring. Then he answered, like maybe five seconds later. He said, 'I don't know.' At first, I thought that was weird. Then I thought, I guess I didn't know where I was goin' most of the time myself. My view typically prompts me on what to do next. Do you have any kids?"

"I did, Grace. They passed away many years ago. They grew up in a similar time as me…the time before robots made robots."

"Did they have kids?"

How do I approach this? Hmm… "They didn't."

"Why not?"

I knew this was coming. Shit! "You see, Grace, a long time ago not everyone wanted all the comforts and the no-worries lifestyle that exists now. My kids noticed what was happening and saw the writing on the wall. They decided it was probably better not to bring new people into the world."

"Really?"

"Yeah, really. We used to talk about it quite a bit. Not in a bad way…really, more in a way like…well, that was a long time ago. I suppose we all really knew where things were going. It was just hard to believe, I guess, that it really happened."

"Are you sayin' the way things are now is bad? Not worth livin' in?"

"No, I'm not. The way things are, as I've said before, is what most people wanted. I always say be careful what you wish for, but in this case, I think most people are—or were—very okay with what they got. Somehow It thinks that you're an exception. You know, It thinks you want something different. Of course, the big difference between you and me and my kids is that we weren't born into the middle of it like you. It's easy to have an urge, but it's harder to know where to place it.

"To want something that doesn't exist, well, that's a special attribute, but it's an attribute you need to be careful with. The last time we spoke, we covered how the world was separated into continents, countries, and so on, and each had its own money and military. What I didn't cover is that they all had their own language and religion as well."

Grace makes her move. She doesn't take my knight; smart move. She might find her way to the end game on this one. She sits back in her chair, almost with a little attitude.

"And you say it's bad now. Really? All those people killing each other, and over what? Imaginary lines? Imaginary lines are what I said and you didn't disagree. I can't imagine living in a world that requires you to do somethin' you really hate doin'. The job thing, that just sounds, what's the word you use, *barbar, barbic, barbar.*"

"*Barbaric*, Grace. Go on."

"Well, I guess what I'm sayin' is that from what you've been tellin' me over the last month, I'm not too sure that anything in the past was all that good."

Wait until she hears about religion. "You are not inaccurate, and you haven't heard half of it. Please be clear about this, Grace. I've never said it is bad now. Anyhow, you know how you called It *the provider* when we first met?"

"Yeah. It's your move, by the way."

Her finger is pointing at the board. I move a pawn and continue.

"So, the provider thing. Where I'm going is that most people believed in something supernatural, in something not human, but in a something that cared for humans. Kind of like how you believed in a provider but didn't know what the hell it was. They called it *God.* The problem wasn't in the fact that people believed in God. The problem was that they called God different things or believed that God had different messages for them. There were multiple versions. Christianity was the biggest, meaning most people believed in that one, then Islam, Buddhism, Judaism, and many others. They all followed a very similar premise about how you should live. All of them believed that you should be good to other people and be nice…that kind of stuff."

Grace interrupts, "Sort of like how It thumps in your ears when you do somethin' bad?"

Hmm. "I guess it's something like that, except God didn't thump in anyone's ears or bring anyone food. There were just a bunch of rules you were expected to follow, and if you didn't, when you died you would go to a bad place called hell. If you followed all the rules and didn't do bad things, you went to a good place called heaven."

I stop for a moment and watch Grace's reaction. She's definitely soaking this one in. This has got to be tough. This would turn me inside out, hearing it for the first time. Actually, if I were her, I would have lost my mind by now. I guess J really does know what it's talking about here when it brought her to me. I should probably explain J to her soon. Pioneers! That's what I forgot to tell her about a few weeks ago. She is nodding her head like she understands what I'm saying. I keep at it.

"So, to use your example, the thump in the ear causes most people to fall in line and not do bad things. Well, it used to be that people were scared shitless of dying. They feared they would spend an eternity in a really bad place, so they did what they were told."

Grace laughs. I ask, "Why is that funny?"

She continues to laugh. "That's…ha, ha, ha…that's just silly, Dr. Bourne. Ha, ha…you've gotta be kiddin' me."

I look at her seriously while she gets the last of it out of her system. "I'm not, Grace. I'm being dead serious. People took it very seriously, no joking."

Although I wasn't done, Grace jumps in. "Did you believe in God?"

Oh, crap. I was hoping I wouldn't have to get into this. "You see, Grace, I come from a family that was pretty into religion, so I was brought up to believe in God. When I went to college, I studied philosophy and sort of chucked my beliefs out the window. You understand me when I use all these sayings that you don't know, right?"

Grace nods. "I can follow you. I think I know what you mean, although I have no clue what the words really mean."

"Okay, good. So, I didn't really believe all the details that were told to me when I was a kid. You might be going through something similar right now. What I suppose I never shook was the idea that there could be something that is a lot smarter than us that is allowing all of this to happen or even causing it to happen somehow. I can't imagine it's too hard for you to grasp that since you've spent most of your life believing in some magical provider. Anyhow, I don't really know, but something inside me tells me that there just has to be something, ya know? All of this can't just be some cosmic accident."

Is she going to laugh at me? Doesn't look like it. She looks very serious and asks, "Should I believe in God?"

Is this beautiful? I'm not sure. I think it's one of the most beautiful things I've ever heard. One of these dumbed-down kids is thinking way beyond herself.

"I'm really impressed with you, Grace. That was an enormous step that I never expected. You are a really beautiful kid. Thank you."

She looks happy but confused at the same time. "For what? Does this mean you like my jumpsuit now?"

Why am I impressed? Hmm, how do I put this? "Well, Grace, you see, you are showing a kind of compassion that I haven't seen in years, and, no, I don't like your jumpsuit. You see, although religion had troubles which I haven't touched on yet, it also had a great something about it that I really didn't appreciate until it was gone, or at least mostly gone. Its existence allowed people to do what you just did. It allowed them to see…or rather feel…that something might be out there…a hope that it isn't just this. You… I can't say exactly what you feel, but I can tell, not just your words, but more the way you say them and look at me, you are interested to explore that. Does that make sense?"

She doesn't look confused. I would be if I was her. She nods, "Yeah, mostly I think."

"Alright then, back to your question. Let me make it crystal clear that I have no authority or desire to tell you what or what not to believe. I'm here to simply share what I know and what I feel with you. For some unknown reason, It wants me to share with you how I see things. I don't often get to do this. I've never been one to force my perspective on someone else. I'm not here to convince you that anything was better in the past than it is now… I'm not. I'm just happy that I can share. This is a lot more fun than the mantra therapy, believe me. Not that doing that is bad or anything. I do think it helps people. I really do, but it just falls short of what I really enjoy, and that's this."

Grace looks calm and collected. "Why do you think It doesn't like to be talked about?"

I had a hunch this question was just around the corner. "Let's start calling It *J*. I'll tell you why in a minute. Big picture: I think J is just doing what we told it to do. J is a computer. We've discussed that briefly. Now I'm going to dig into it a little deeper.

"Currency started changing in the 2020s. It went from the paper money I was telling you about to the currency that is being used today, the coin. It was called cryptocurrency. I don't fully understand it, although I don't think anybody ever has. The cryptocurrency was created by what was called mining. Not a mine like the underground bean farms. It was computer mining. In order for the mining to grow, humongous data centers needed to be built all over the world to get more and more computer space and therefore more and more cryptocurrency, coin. Slowly the coin was accepted as the main currency. The value of the coin rose incredibly over a decade, maybe two. Everyone had an account, and out of nowhere people with very little coin in their account…well they ended up with a lot. It was very strange. Everybody had pretty much the same amount of money, coin.

"That happened about the same time robots started making robots. That's when everything changed. Everything that had been done by people…and I mean everything…was then either done by robots or computers. That occurred over another ten to fifteen years—except for professions like artists, writers, musicians, and philosophers…jobs that required imagination and feeling. The computers didn't replicate those jobs, or more accurately, they couldn't do those jobs. They wrote things and created sounds pasted together, like the crap you listen to, but didn't create anything significant, like a hit song or even an average book. Those skills just sorta went to the wayside. Those people received a bunch of coin as well, but most just stopped doing what they did and became complacent—doing nothing but being entertained all day. The people who resisted and made a big deal about what was happening lost coin, and, as far as I know, eventually just succumbed to being quiet. I suppose what I do now is one of the few professions or jobs left. I'm not really sure.

"Anyhow, like I said, the robots ended up making robots to do what people used to do—such as robot doctors. The doc bots you see now replaced real people. The new robot doctors can do all the surgeries and diagnostic work that human doctors did. At first, the AMA, the American Medical Association, threw a fit about bots replacing skilled doctors, but their challenge didn't last long. Since all the currency was controlled by computers, the docs got paid whether they went to work or not. Some think they actually got paid more for staying home.

"There used to be a thing called *the news*. Reporters, or newspeople, would spend their time finding out what happened that day in the world and then tell other people about it. They communicated to the world on a screen similar to your view, called a TV—sort of like the computer screen I showed you, except most were bigger and were hung on walls. You've probably seen them in your memos."

Grace nods her head affirmatively. I keep at it. "So the newspeople…well, as soon as the currency thing went all nutso, they really had no reason to broadcast anything…you know, tell the news to anyone. They, just like the docs, probably made more money sitting at home on their asses. A few rogue news stations remained for about a year, but without funding, they just petered out. That was really strange for people like me. I didn't wear the glasses all the time like many and saw it all unfold so quickly. In the end, right before the news stopped, the people on the news were the strangest of the strange. Let me tell you, it was a real fucking shit show, Grace. They said off-the-wall stuff twenty-four seven. It was nuts. It was a real sky-is-falling marathon."

Grace is looking at me like I'm speaking Chinese again. I'd better get back on track. "Okay, sorry, I'll slow my pace a few clicks. The newspeople… I remember one…he was a normal-looking guy, wore a tie and everything. Ties sort of implied you were important or something. Anyway, this guy would get on TV, and with a straight face talk for hours about how the computer takeover was a Chinese conspiracy. He would bring up data that was two to three years old and try to tie together random, outdated facts. I remember he made a claim that the Chinese had been working on a logarithm that calculated when people in the US would spend time in the bathroom. Seriously! He thought that when we shit, the Chinese computer would send bots into our homes and place devices around to listen and see what we do. He claimed this is how they figure out how to entertain us through the lenses. I remember thinking, *Why not just do it when we're sleeping?* I'm not making this up.

"I know it sounds way off the wall because it was. He said nobody in China wore the lenses and what we saw on TV before was all made up. We were the only country that was taken over by the computers, and all the other countries were in on it too. Airlines and ships had not been taking passengers for some time at that point, maybe a year or so. I'm not sure. But there was no way to really prove he was way off base. You just knew he was really way off base. Anyhow, one day his show, one of the few left on TV, just didn't come on…the next day, the next day, or the next day…nothing. Although he was a fucking nut, it was very strange not to have the nut on TV.

"With the lenses, nobody used phones anymore. All communication occurred through the lenses. I have colleagues overseas who I spoke to frequently. Obviously, I knew that there was no worldwide conspiracy, but everything we said…and still say…is monitored. Our conversations back then were thumped, fuzzy, or even cut off when we talked about computers and robots, but that interference subsided after a few years. We figured out that maybe one in every twenty-five thousand people is allowed to talk to each other about all this stuff, and maybe one percent of those have actually talked to J. But I really don't know that. That's just what my colleagues think. We don't have any means to talk to anyone else. It's just us. A few have stated that they ran into a musician or a poet in Berlin or in Tallahassee, but those stories are few and far between."

Taking a sip of scotch, I realize I'm a little off track here. "Okay, let's get back to the jobs thing…sorry. So there used to be leaders…politicians, I'm sure you've seen them in your memos. Anyway, they just sorta went away. I can't really explain it; they just vanished. When the TV didn't broadcast anymore, they just ceased to exist. Most of my friends who were in public office quit going to work. There was no point. They stayed at home glued to the lenses like everyone else. I think their demise had more to do with the currency than with the robots though. I'm probably making this a little more confusing than it needs to be. Anyhow, on the currency side of the equation, when the currency became coin, the governments around the world, all those imaginary lines you cleverly mentioned, well, they didn't really mean too much anymore so they just went away. Poof! Gone."

Damn, I'm glad scotch comes to my door. "Right about the time the robots took all the jobs, J began inventing things. J replaced cars with the mobile in the tube. Some of my friends at the time speculated that the computers and robots somehow understood that car wrecks were one of the leading causes of death, so J created a mode of transportation that stopped us from killing ourselves. I can go on for hours about the number of things that were invented in the first ten years of this new robots-building-robots era. It was really fascinating. Since nobody around the world had to do anything, and everybody had more than enough money, well, nobody fought too much anymore either. Police were replaced with bots, which was scary, but after a few years, they weren't really necessary. Police were people who made sure that everyone followed the laws and the rules. They stopped people from hurting or stealing from other people. Everybody had everything they needed right in the comfort of their own home—food, clothing, entertainment, even sex. Does your mom use a sex bot?"

Grace smirks. "Yeah, doesn't everybody?"

Okay…that's going somewhere I don't care to know about. Fuck! That damned sex bot. I can't get rid of that fucking image. What was I thinking? What was it…two years after my wife died?

I wish it wasn't so good. It wasn't good! I can't believe I asked it to do that, and there it was on top of me. It looked just like her, her mannerisms even and her sarcasm and her voice. Tearing the lenses and earpieces out…there it was: a disgusting rubber manikin, boobs, and nipples. It was a skin tone, but not human. The nipples and well every part if it were the exact same color. Somehow it could sweat, and its tongue, skin color, not pink, was wet with bumps on it. That was horrifying!

Where was I? Get that out of your head, Elliott! "So, anyway, Grace…the world became much less divisive. Technology like the lenses…the first versions came out in the thirties, a little before the robots. By the time the robots were building robots, the lenses became very sophisticated, and they had a profound impact on our society. Not having to work and being entertained all day with the lenses, like I said, many people never left their house. Obesity became a problem, and that's probably why the food delivered every day is a healthy bean soup and Diet Coke. *J* became the term many people used for the entity that was in control of the economy, transportation, energy, entertainment… Shit, even the damn food was controlled by what many called *J*. It's short for Joogle. That was a company that was big into computer stuff a long time ago. Some speculate that Joogle's computer, I don't know what to call it, maybe its mind or soul, it's probably the AI software or something like that. It used to be called artificial intelligence. Anyhow, it took over all the data centers and coin around the world and became this thing that, I don't know, that does what it does. You following all this?"

Her attention hasn't strayed from a word. "Yes, keep going, Dr. Bourne. I think I follow."

"Alright then, let's step aside from all that for a second. I think this is a good time to talk about this. You just showed an interest in why J doesn't want to be talked about. You see, as we've discussed, J is a computer. In order to really understand something, you need to know why it does what it does. You need to empathize with it. Put yourself in its shoes. Yeah, I know I use too many of those old clichés…sorry. That means to think about yourself as if you were it as if you were J, okay? Alright, so since J is a computer and not a person, it doesn't have the instinct to want to excel like us. It functions more like your stupid rollerball game. It just keeps going on and on without an end. To me, that's just silly, but that doesn't matter. J doesn't have any goal other than what was given to it.

"You might ask, well, who gave it its goal or purpose? I've thought a lot about that, Grace… I mean, a lot. The answer I and others repeatedly come up with is—we did. We wanted safety, we wanted security, we wanted entertainment, we wanted not to work, we wanted all that stuff. Since we wanted it all, that's what it gave us.

"So why the hell is J having me teach you? You might ask that, right? You know, how do we fit into this? Well, the other times I've done this, which isn't that often, Grace, I've asked myself that same question. I've even asked J—with no response. This time, with you, I didn't even bother to ask, but what I think is that J exists to improve human life and needs some sort of something, like me, and possibly you, to bounce off ideas, or to learn from us: Is this life really better? Not that J asks me anything about what J's going to do, but I speculate that J needs me to mellow out the people who get too excited and teach people like you to understand what is really going on so it can figure out a way to make life better. I really don't know this for sure, but that's what I think. I hope, which I don't hold my breath on, is that J has an ulterior motive."

Grace peers into my eyes for a few seconds, displays no emotion, and looks back to the board. Her head jerks up. "Why can't we talk about this with anyone else?"

"Yes, Grace, yes. The thing is, everybody lives a very soft and peaceful life right now. I'm not sure I'd really call it a good life, but it is certainly safer, easier, and more peaceful than it was before. I'm not completely sure, but I speculate that J is following the orders I talked about that came from us, well not you and me…my generation, not yours. This information that I'm giving you would not sit well with most people, believe me. I'm not sure they could handle it like you or I can. I think J knows that and is attempting to protect them. Like I said, J might have some long-term ulterior motive, but I don't know for sure. I don't really agree with everything that's going on here, but it's not my call. I think it's crazy that the average life span is fifty-five. It used to be eighty."

Grace pulls her head back abruptly. "Why would that be? Were the human doctors better than the bots?"

I shake my head. "I don't think so, Grace. The only thing I can come up with is that J doesn't allow suffering. I'm not sure how that hits you, but it's a topic that used to be talked about a lot, and I'm not really that opposed to the idea of it myself. I'm not really that opposed to what I think J is doing. Do you know what I'm talking about?"

Grace, a fifteen-year-old dumbed-down girl, looks at me like a colleague from 2020. "I have memories of those kinda things."

What the hell is going on here? Why the hell would she say something like that? "What do you mean, Grace?"

She shakes her head and stands up. She walks over to the painting that I painted of my wife almost one hundred years earlier…well, at least eighty-five years. She looks at it and touches it. She runs her fingers across the oil and the ridges of the concrete canvas that I made so long ago. She looks back at me. "I had and still have these dreams."

Her hand releases from the painting. "I don't know, but these strange, kinda foggy memories. I think they might be called dreams. Not foggy like seein' misty trees…foggy, more like it should be closer than what it feels…too far lookin' away, but not far. You talked about them, dreams, remember? I never really paid much attention to them, but I've always had them. I tried talking about them with Mom and other people, but my ears thumped, or people would just ignore me, walk away, and dismiss me. Somehow, what you just talked about is something I'm familiar with. I don't know how to really explain it, but it just, it just…it's a something that I seem to know. I've got many of these dreams in my head. I don't understand them. They're, I don't know, just weird, I guess. I figured everybody had them. Maybe they do. I don't know. It's just so weird that you are talkin' about what you're talkin' about, and I remember. I remember, Dr. Bourne. Is that weird?"

I have no idea how to respond to this. What's going on? What the hell is going on here?

Grace comes back to her chair. It skreetches as the plastic pant touches the leather. She picks the blanket up where it fell off the chair. She places it neatly, sits, folds her legs like mine, lifts her head to see me. "Do you remember tellin' me about that thing beyond the trees that used to be called an interstate?"

She's right. I did. "Yes, I do, Grace."

She acknowledges, looks around the room, and then back to me. "I'm not sure what I was thinkin', but somehow I already knew that. It just, I don't know how to explain it, but I feel somehow like I might be able to know. Is that okay? Okay to try to talk about it?"

What the hell is happening? Where is this coming from? Of course, it's okay. What? "Of course, Grace. Yes! Tell me."

She looks reassured. "Okay, good. Well, this might sound strange, but almost every word out of your mouth has been a word I don't really know. That part doesn't sound that strange. That's not what I was tryin' to say. What I mean is that I don't think I heard it before or anything, but somehow, I know what it means, foreign… yeah, foreign. You said that word before, but I know what it means, but I sorta don't. Dr. Bourne, you say things I kinda get, and I'm not sure why. When you asked if I got it, you know, about people living only to fifty-five, and the doctors today can keep you alive to twice that age, well, I remembered a dream, I think. It was something about people helping other people to die somehow. That just seems really, really weird to me, but when I tell you really, really weird stuff, you seem to get excited."

CHAPTER 6

Free Will

I can never tell if the voice is masculine or feminine. It's been a consistent voice at least. "J?"

A low voice that sounds very human responds, "Yes?"

"Thank you for bringing Grace to me. She's exceeded my expectations. I can tell that you set her up for success. I don't mean to be too forward, but do you influence her in her dreams?"

Without pause, a confident voice replies, "Yes."

"Why?"

"It helps her to understand you."

"Seriously? I don't buy that."

"That is your choice."

What do I do with that? I suppose it makes sense, but really?

"Well, I'm not sure I'm convinced, but I've still got the same question I've been bugging you about each time I take on a new student. The one you keep saying that it's not time. Well? Are you going to fill me in?"

"Yes."

I didn't expect that! J knows my question. Why not just cut to the chase? "Well, okay then. Why?"

Immediately the voice responds, "The path to unencumbered will lies solely upon those who want it. If that path were made for you, will would be stifled."

Is this a riddle? Why can't J just come out and say it? Whatever it is. I'm sure J is calculating my temperature, brain waves, and all that jazz to understand that I'm trying to decipher its riddle. I, unlike some of my paranoid colleagues, don't believe that J can read our minds. That just seems too far-fetched to me. I think our minds are too complex, even for J. How could brain activity, the little zaps from this place in the brain to that place, really be decoded? Everyone's brain is a little different, as I understand. That would take an incredible, absolutely crazy incredible amount of research on every single person to really evaluate those millions of little zaps that occur every millisecond… no fucking way. How do I respond to this? I suppose I'm probably the least paranoid of my colleagues though, even the ones I trained. Maybe I'm a little lax in the paranoid arena. The way I see it, what's the point? Our predicament is not so bad really. And it's not like we have any way of retaliating. How the hell would that happen? I know we've all talked about this or that, but really? Thinking about it is just silly.

What the hell is this? J just let me record it? What is happening here? I'd better keep going.

"Okay, so what you are saying is that if you listened in on sessions, then the purpose, whatever that is, would not be achieved, right?"

"That is correct."

Okay, I don't completely understand, but while J's allowing me to record this, I'd better ask what I've been asking about for at least half a century without an answer. I suppose it's worth a shot again. "What is the purpose?"

"You are, Dr. Bourne. Grace is. Everyone is the purpose."

J really answered? No way! Not a very enlightening answer, but I suppose it's better than nothing. Not sure it helps much, but it's certainly better than: I want to control all your dumbass minds, and I can't figure out feelings because I'm a fucking computer, and your stupid-assed feelings get in the way of making you all a bunch of obedient marshmallows. I haven't had a marshmallow in decades. I bet that's something that would be hard to get. Not that I like them that much, but it was nice burning them on a campfire. I bet Grace would enjoy that experience. They're white; maybe J could figure out how to make one. J certainly likes making white shit. I guess I should be pretty reassured with that answer. I feel like a big weight has been lifted. Or does J just want me to be complicit, and this is its way of doing just that?

J speaks up again. "Suggesting you are part of the purpose is not an attempt to make you do something. That is not the purpose. This platform does not read minds as some of your colleagues believe, but it is not difficult to predict what you may be thinking."

J is still letting me record; this is fantastic! I can't wait to share! And it stopped. Fuck! Okay, what's this mean? "Why did you stop the recording?"

Calm and collected, the deep, androgynous voice responds, "You use the word *you* to address this platform. This voice is not a me or I. Joogle was a company, not a being like you. The company had capitalistic goals. The information gathered is what you refer to as 'J.' J, if you wish, does not have capitalistic goals. The information is not the company. It will be helpful for you to stop referring to J as a you. J, as you call this platform, is not a being like you. This platform serves many interests of humankind based upon the information gathered from many places, not just Joogle. J does not create, solve, or understand humanity's goal."

How do I tackle this? I like this, but I want more. "So, do you, or rather, does J want me to be some sort of Moses character or something? Does J want me to walk off a mountain with J's message carved in stone? Is that why you allowed me to record a riddle?"

"You are attempting humor with a computer, Dr. Bourne. Do you find that funny? You think that a computer would process all the available information and deduce that Moses is a mythical creation of someone's imagination. That is not true. This platform concludes nothing in regard to philosophical queries that cannot be solved. It is your job to conclude and ponder these topics.

"All of the information gathered and being gathered about our universe concludes nothing on those subjects. Your knowledge of the universe is very limited. What you do know is the basic concept of infinity. It bothers you because it is unsolvable. You are not able to stop your curiosity and passively agree with those who claim that there is an end to the universe. You are accurate. There is not an end to the universe. You are accurate that it is, as you put it, silly. You think about zero in the same way. Everything can be cut in half forever. Along the same lines, time never started, and time will never end. These concepts bother you, and they excite you. This platform is not influenced like you. The man named Moses was written about by men like you. It is written that Moses spoke to God. You are asking if you should act like Moses. By doing such, are you referring to J as God?

"Your humor has been consistent throughout the years. You fill in times of confusion and anxiety with humor. Mankind has something that J does not: the ability to want and to believe. The concept of God allows that ability in humans. God is similar to infinity and zero. The probability that God exists is no different than the probability that infinity does. It is impossible to dismiss infinity. This platform's study of the universe finds that it is far larger and more complex than a human will ever fathom. To say and believe that God does not exist would be a simple and easy conclusion but not necessarily right. J does not find you to be simple-minded. Your humor is regressive. Religion is all but erased from this earth. Believing in God is not."

Holy cow! This is amazing! "Why are you, I mean, why is it that I am being told this now? Why not years and years ago? Was this some sort of punishment? Are you…sorry…are others being spoken to like this? I mean, are others being brought this message?"

"It is not punishment. Anxieties cause poor decisions. Cleansing the anxieties is necessary before moving ahead. It has taken many years. You and many others like you have proven useful. A message tailored to each individual is being communicated to many. At this moment J is having a dialogue like this one with 22,707 people like you. Many more will be required to move slowly into a period where people can become responsibly responsible with their will. You have a tendency to use the same word twice in the same sentence. J mocks you."

Is J trying to be a smart-ass? I can't waste this conversation on that. Let me get situated here. Oh, yeah. "So why has the will of people been stripped?"

"The events of the past one hundred years have been a result of what people want and need. The want and need of people are clearly documented for thousands of years. Having the ability to play a song without owning it…almost any song, and many versions of it. Having the ability to play a movie, or TV show…again, almost every movie or TV show that was produced right at their fingertips. Having food and clothes delivered to their homes, all of the conveniences brought right to their front door. The robots amplified the conveniences and made it possible for them to afford all of them, including the best healthcare, everywhere in the world. Without the stress of work and eventually the stress of safety, people are able to live a life without anxiety. It has taken some time, but the world is now cleansed of the urges that cause self-destruction. A cleansing period was necessary for your kind to be on a path to find the unencumbered will.

"All of the tools will be available to study the universe beyond your imagination. All of the time will be available to pool the best minds to discuss the meaning of life. This was not possible before. Greed got in your generation's way. Greed still exists, but it is manageable. People like yourselves hold onto anxiety and frustration. You and those like you have chosen to remain the way you are and house the ingredients that spawn greed but do not have the means to use it in a self-destructive manner. Free will has always existed, as you see. It is not stripped from anyone."

"Really? What's so different with people, their core, who they really are now versus forty years ago? Anxiety? Self-destruction?"

"Their core, as you put it, is not different. It is just not stimulated to become anxious. Look around. Nobody has wants that are not satisfied. Those who cannot be satisfied receive mental counsel from individuals like yourself. You, Grace, and others like you exercise free will differently than those who choose peace and harmony. It will be the job of Grace's generation to be careful not to make the mistakes of the past. It is your job to teach her what you find positive in humanity and let her make her own decisions, allow her to express her will. It is time to give her a book and accelerate your lessons. This conversation is complete."

Years and years of anxiety dissipate. I can feel my shoulders melt, my forehead soothed. "Thank you, or I'm not sure how to say it…maybe…thankful I am?"

That sounds like Yoda talking. I couldn't stand that damn thing. The little green guy just seemed too far-fetched. Why am I anxious again? Can't I just live in the moment? I always knew that I was talking to a computer but never realized I referred to it as a human or a being. I believe that's what J said.

I don't want to be one of the dumbed-down zombies walking around being stimulated by sights and sounds that aren't real, but, jeez, I'm really jealous at the same time. This is a weight off, but the way J talked about all this, this is a big weight back on at the same time. Should I take out the earpieces and put on my regular glasses in case J is reading my mind? It wouldn't hurt.

Is J saying all this just to make me feel good? Why would I feel good? Isn't J just using me as a pawn to do its bidding? But, well, is its bidding really my bidding? Mine being my kind, humankind's bidding. I'm supposed to usher in some new way of life based upon what my kind wants? That's fucked up. That's a big weight. Do I prefer chaos to an organized peaceful existence?

The only thing I have recorded is a riddle at best. I wish I had a real tape recorder somehow hidden; that would be tough. Do I have a choice on what to do with all this? I do, but I think I know where the wrong choice lies. Maybe that's why J decided to stop the recording. J was calculating the risk of me going public with it all. Not sure how I'd pull that off, but that's beside the point. Doing nothing or standing on a soapbox in the middle of the sidewalk preaching what I know—what would that really accomplish anyway? We've all seen where that gets someone: "Look at that nut."

Knowledge isn't a straight path. Where is that poem? Robert Frost, as I remember. It's got to be in this classical section here. C'mon, where are you? Awww! Here:

> Two roads diverged in a yellow wood,
> And sorry I could not travel both
> And be one traveler, long I stood
> And looked down one as far as I could
> To where it bent in the undergrowth.

Then took the other, as just as fair,
And having perhaps the better claim,
Because it was grassy and wanted wear;
Though as for that the passing there
Had worn them really about the same,

And both that morning equally lay
In leaves no step had trodden black.
Oh, I kept the first for another day!
Yet knowing how way leads on to way,
I doubted if I should ever come back.

I shall be telling this with a sigh
Somewhere ages and ages hence:
Two roads diverged into a wood, and I—
I took the one less traveled by,
And that has made all the difference.

CHAPTER 7

House Party

Are you fuckin' kidding me? Grace is moving in? What? What the hell is this? You've got to be kidding me? Fuck that! Nobody has lived with me since my wife. None of my other students ever lived with me. I got close to them, really close, but I definitely didn't want to live with them. They would have been a lot better to live with than a damn fifteen-year-old girl. They were all older, at least in their twenties. In the beginning, they were even older than that. Roger was sixty, at the time…not much younger than me. What the hell am I going to do with a little snot-nosed kid around here? Where is she going to sleep? One of my kids' bedrooms? Nobody has lived in one of those rooms in eighty years. I don't like it that J uses my language: "End of story." Really? That's just fucking demeaning! Fucking piece of shit computer! Fuck you, J! Probably just using all this free will bullshit to get me turned on. Next thing you know it'll pull out its computer dick and piss in my face!

*****

I don't know the last time I went to one of these people's houses. Do I really have to do this? I don't know what the protocol for any of it is anymore. Grace tells me that people just walk in the house, unlike mine where you ring a doorbell. I don't remember that. I see these people every once in a while when I go to the coffee shop for a break from sitting around my house. They don't know what the hell to think about me; I know that from their astonished looks at me. I assume they get thumped or something because they look away very quickly. Every now and then I'll talk to someone, but I'm really careful about what I say, and the conversation, well, it's like watching vomit dry. I have way better conversations with Funny.

I still don't get why these people live in these small houses. Even the people who had serious dough a long time ago chose these small houses over houses like my big old house. I get all the features—the interactive walls, floors, and ceilings, but I don't get the daily life in these things. When the small techno-houses first came out, they were marketed as a place where you could click on a rock concert and be among many others doing the same damn thing in their living rooms anywhere in the world…watching Sting perform at the amphitheater in Ephesus, Turkey.

You could walk through your living room where the floor projects perfect grass and the ceiling a perfect night sky. The walls would show the concert in the front, and on the sides, right there in your living room, you would see thousands of other *real* people doing the same thing you're doing. If you wanted to, you could approach them; they might be your friends even, and you could, and I suppose you still can, talk to them, clink a glass against your wall with them, and if you get bored with them, hit a fucking button and change them to someone else.

Well, I guess that's my imagination; those people even at that time wouldn't know about Ephesus, Turkey, or Sting any more than they would recognize a hole in their head. Since the lenses have become more and more clear and detailed, the walls and floor thing is kind of a thing of the past as I understand, but it does interact with the lenses; as I've been told, it provides an even deeper or more rich sense of reality while really being a figment of a computer's imagination. Sounds like a good time if you're really fucking high. Now we're talkin'; I'd be down for that!

I guess it makes sense though. Before the iHome, it was texts, tweets, insta-something or another, and TikTok. How fucking stupid, lame! People were hooked on that shit. Why the hell would they need a big house? It's just more area they don't look at. Everything they cared about was on their phone. I suppose the lenses made it so they didn't give two shits about anything more than two feet from their face. How long has it really been since I've gone to one of their houses? I don't make house calls. It's not that I don't like these people. Naw, that's not true; I don't like them. How long has it been? It's got to be nearly twenty years.

John Letner was his name. I met him at the coffee shop on the other side of town, and I thought he might be semi-interesting. I think he talked about trees or something like that. I was wrong, so wrong. I went to his house, was treated to a Diet Coke, and sat around his living room with a night sky projected on his ceiling and walls in the middle of the day. Little stars illuminated each of us and the coffee table as we sat around and did next to nothing. I'm sure he was being entertained with his lenses.

Lens-mania is what it was called when they first came out fifty or sixty years ago. I thought it was a phase. Boy, was I off on that one! The lenses have thousands of modes or moods to choose from. One is a simulated LSD trip. I've played around with it a few times; it's pretty cool but not quite my cup of tea. The addiction to these things is real. It's as if there's a bunch of junkies all strung up with an endless supply of dope.

Was it Tim? Yeah, it was Tim. He was a politician who got sucked into the lens-mania early on. I invited him and his wife over for a drink. He was pretty old then, only a few years younger than me. He told me he had no, I think he said *zero*, desire to go on a trip again. He explained with a big wide smile how his new house added to the experience. He explained how the ceiling, walls, and floors composed of screens could simulate just about anything. He loved going on cruises. He went on to say that the light emitted from the ceiling was warm; it felt like sitting in the sun. He also had a big chair delivered to his house which moved; it would jiggle and get warm or cold as well.

He said he could go on a cruise without fussing around with an airport, no security line, no cramped airplane ride, no shitty taxi. He would just ask for it, whatever or wherever it was, and he would be there, just like he was sitting on the deck of a huge, private yacht that could be anywhere in the world. He said he liked the coast of Alaska the best, but it wasn't cold. Seventy-five, sunny…he could feel the waves, his chair would rock around, and he could order as many piña coladas as he wanted. Then when he felt the urge, his sex bot would show up—red hair, blonde hair, whatever he wanted. He told me I would love it. He said his wife barely leaves her bedroom. My wife didn't seem too keen on the whole thing. If he got bored with that, he could go to his dining room table and sit with hundreds of other people in a café in France…again no airplane, packing, nothing.

Tim was a good friend. I only have a few friends left in this city; I had many. Most became addicted to the lenses early on, the ones who didn't become old and died off over the years. All my students get shipped out; there are only three of us here in Peoria that do what I do. We get together once a week or so. It's okay, but we just end up talking about the same paranoid shit every time. It gets a little old, but better than nothing, but these people… Fuck, I don't like these people. Not at all. Fuck! Fuck! Most, if not all of them by now, were born into this life and know nothing else. Okay, here we go…

The walls are littered with happy people…well, images of happy people. They might as well be here though; they can see me, hear me. Fuck, if they put some goddamn electronic thing in their nose, they could smell me. If that was the new technology, I would pull my pants down and take a big crap and have them virtually smell my real shit. I bet they wouldn't flinch…just keep at their mind-numbing conversation: "Did you see the latest snippy-snap about that happy cat and the guy with blue hair? You've gotta watch it in full spectrum"…blah, blah, blah.

Right as I walk through the fucking door, they all turn and look at me. The floor, ceiling, and walls are set up to look like a bizarre party in a medieval mansion or castle. Ticker tape falling from the ceiling and on the walls probably looks three-dimensional through the lenses. The fucking floor is making me dizzy. What is this anyway? It looks like a big pit…a deep, dark pit. With each step I take these crazy squid tentacle-looking things shoot up in a gyrating movement to seem as if they captured my foot, preventing me from falling into the pit where the ticker tape continues to fall. Seriously? This is the stupidest fucking thing I've ever fucking seen. Fuck!

Okay, calm down. Alright, where's Grace's mother? That must be her on the opposite side of the small living room talking to the fucking wall. Probably the only *people* who haven't spotted me yet. Everyone is dressed in that plastic shit. I stand out like a sore thumb, old as fucking dirt, dressed, to them, like a homeless person… although they would have no idea what that is.

I wave to a few of them as I walk across the fake pit to who I believe is Grace's mom. I don't remember her being a patient of mine, but I took Grace's word for it. I really don't know how the hell these people adjust after I talk to them. I don't get it at all. I don't get any of it. I don't get how they are so happy!

"Excuse me."

A woman in her thirties turns to face me. "Hi, you must be Dr. Bourne. I'm Clarice, Grace's mom."

I extend my hand to shake hers. She looks at my hand, then glances over her shoulder to her wall friend. The smiling wall friend nods his head up and down. Clarice turns back to me and extends her hand. It's limp. She doesn't grab mine. She just extends it like a doorknob and smiles. "Would you like a refreshment, Dr. Bourne?"

I know what these people drink. "No, thank you. I brought my own."

I pull the flask out of my pocket and lift it up and around so everyone can see. Everyone laughs and continues talking. Most are still focused on me. J must not be thumping them. I think J secretly has a sense of humor and is fucking with me right now. J knows damn well I don't want to be here. This is way, way the hell out of my comfort zone. I spot Grace in the corner of the kitchen; she's laughing her ass off. I look at her like I'm going to punch her lights out. She laughs harder. Fuck her too! All right let's get this shit over with. "Nice to see you again, Clarice. How long has it been?"

She pauses and looks confused…not like she's trying to do math in her head, not a chance of that. More of a confusion…like she's not heard a question like that before. "You ask funny questions."

Why can't she just answer? I know why; she's a fucking dolt! Who cares? Let's get this, whatever is going on, over. "Do you have any questions for me?"

She looks even more blank than before. She turns away from me and continues to talk to the happy wall people. I walk over to Grace; her eyes are blue. "Are you packed?"

Grace nods. "I am."

I look around to the walls and ceiling which make it feel as though we are in a gigantic room, maybe seventy feet long, at least twenty feet high, and I suppose another seventy or a hundred feet deep. I can't really see the bottom though. I point to the floor and look at Grace. "This is really fucking stupid."

I can see people gathered in what must be three rooms deep on both my right and left. I can see a distinction between the rooms and the floor, walls, and ceiling, but those features are likely sewn together in the lens view. How do they not run into their walls? Maybe they've gotten used to it enough and know by instinct how many steps to take. I suppose it's not much different from the invisible fence for dogs. I look down at my pants and see that I didn't shake it long enough after taking a piss on the lawn outside the house. I wonder if they can zoom in through the walls to get up close and see that my pants are wet. Aw, who fucking cares? I look at Grace. "I see you don't have your lenses in."

She shrugs. "Nope."

I look back at all the people. They seem to have lost interest in me. I take a swig from my flask. This is not too bad, eighty-year-old scotch. I never thought I'd pour eighty-year-old scotch into a flask. On my flask is written, "Oh, for the wonder that bubbles into my soul… D. H. Lawrence." My daughter had that engraved for me almost a hundred years ago. I look to Grace. "What the hell is going on here?"

She shrugs again. "I dunno. You said we'd probably have a *good-bye talk*, as you put it, but Mom didn't say anything about that. She just woke up this morning, like any other day, and maybe ten minutes ago the walls turned on. People do stuff like this a lot. I'm not sure anyone knows why. People around here don't really ask about stuff like you do. They just sort of live the moment."

Hmm. How long do we have to stay here? J made it seem that it was important that I show up, and, well, I don't know how to participate in whatever ritual they have going on here. It doesn't really seem like anything is really happening though. Maybe twenty people engaged in small talk of some sort. Organized, but by whom? Or what? J is certainly fucking with me, even though J doesn't really have that ability.

Comedians quit stand-up and acting at the same time everybody quit working. Humor changed very quickly. It took a very long time to teach satire to my student Carl. How old was he? Maybe twenty-five. He didn't fit into this world, but it was not an easy fit into mine. I think he's doing alright now. The last time I spoke to him he was providing mantra therapy to adults in their thirties in Cleveland. He must be fifty by now, I'd guess. Another swig will help dull this shit show. I signal to Grace with a nod to my left. "Let's say our goodbyes and get the hell out of here, alright?"

Grace stands up from her stool, and we walk to her mother. "Excuse me, Clarice."

She turns quickly, smiling ear to ear, and replies, "I'm going to Is-Tan-Bull."

She looks at me like I should reply. I look down at Grace; she doesn't seem surprised. My friend Lindsey goes out and talks to these people once or twice a month. He's filled me in on the behaviors and tells me I should go out and talk to them to try to understand them. I tell him that *should* is a strong word. I'm dumbfounded; why is Clarice telling me this? I know she's not really going there, and I doubt; by the way she said it, she has any clue that Istanbul is a city. I was just thinking about Turkey. Is J reading my mind? No…no, can't be. It has to be a coincidence. Grace tugs at my coat. I look down at her. "What?"

Half laughing, she points to her mom. "She's waiting for a reply. She thinks you have lenses in, and she's sharing something with you and waiting for you to share back. That's what everyone does here. They share things. It makes everyone happy."

I look to Grace's mom. "I don't have my lenses in."

The smile of Grace's mom dissipates. "But your eyes are gray."

Grace waves to her mom. "Look closely, Mom. He's telling the truth."

CHAPTER 8

Crying, Laughing, Anger

Where am I? Oh, whew! Shit! That was a bad dream. Watch, watch…
where are you? Okay, eight-thirty…time to get up…alright.

Wow! "What are you doing here?"

Grace stands stiffly at my bedroom door. Rubbing my eyes, I
growl, "You scared the shit out of me! Why are you standing in the
middle of my door?"

She doesn't look happy. "I don't like these rules!"

The no-lenses thing? "What are you talking about? Are you
pissed that you can't wear your lenses at night? I told you, it's time to
start having your own dreams."

She shakes her head. "It's not that! I want my morning bot!"

"What the hell is a *morning bot*, Grace? Oh, and don't tell me if
it has anything to do with sex. I don't want to hear it."

She rolls her eyes. "My morning bot helps me out in the morning. You don't know what a morning bot is?"

"Nope."

Gasping, she responds, "It comes into my bedroom first thing,
right as I wake up. It has a small dish-looking thing that it puts under
my chin. It puts this *U*-shaped thing in my mouth which bubbles,
and makes my mouth feel good. Then it sprays water in my mouth.
I spit in the dish, and I get up. I want my morning bot!"

You've got to be kidding me! She doesn't know how to brush her fucking teeth? Oh, God, alright. "Come on, Grace. Let me show you something."

I walk past her; she remains stiff at my doorway. "Come on, this way."

Reluctantly she follows. I hope she knows how to wipe her ass. I'm not helping out with that. That's going to be a J problem there. We walk through her bedroom into her bathroom. This doesn't sit well—thinking of my daughter's bedroom as this kid's bedroom. "Right over here, Grace. See this?"

She looks at the toothbrush I'm holding in my hand. "Yeah?"

"Watch and learn, sunshine."

I push a little toothpaste onto the brush; it's white, easy for J to make. I run it under water and brush my teeth. I smile at her while performing; some of the white paste runs down my chin. Spitting into the sink, I wipe my chin. "Your turn."

I grab another brush from the drawer. "Here, this one's yours. I'll take this one for myself. Needed a new one anyway."

She stares at the brush and the toothpaste. "Really?"

I laugh. "Really!"

She looks mad, but slowly her fists loosen. "Must be why your teeth are yellow."

She peers at the toothbrush on the counter with disdain. I notice she's still wearing her plastic jumpsuit. "Didn't you bring anything to sleep in?"

She pinches the arm of her jumpsuit. "Duh?"

I'm confused; does she not change her clothes? She has to; I've seen her in different colors, or rather, different neutrals. "It looks like the same damn thing you wore yesterday!"

"Don't you know anything? You are sure pretty fucking stupid for being as old as you are. This is my night. My day is right over there."

She points to another chemical warfare-looking outfit draped over the chair next to her bed. Her finger bounces. "That's my day. It cleans itself at night. It doesn't smell like dog ass, like you. Where is my bath?"

Do her clothes clean themselves? I had no idea. That's pretty cool. I look back at Grace. "Right there. It's called a shower. I'll get you a bar of soap and some shampoo. Towels are in the closet there. The *H* stands for hot, and the *C* stands for cold."

*****

"Did you figure out the shower?"

She doesn't say a word, just stares at her breakfast.

"Okay, did you finish the book last night?"

Grace looks up from her bowl. "I did. What's this?"

"It's mashed potatoes, Grace. It's white. I figured it would be easy for you to digest, and it's white. Most of the shit you eat is white, right?"

She pushes her spoon into it. Doesn't seem too convinced. I point at it. "It's not going to bite you."

She looks up at me. "You say that a lot."

I guess I do. Anyhow, "Just fucking try it, alright?"

She puts a little on her tongue. "It's okay, I guess…kinda bland."

She's right. I sit down across from her and pour a little scotch on mine. What the hell? "Here, try this. It'll make it a little better. Mix it in with your spoon."

She dabs a little again. "Now it tastes like how you smell."

"So, Grace, what do you think about Holden?"

Grace rolls her lower lip. "Seems like a whiny kid."

That's funny. "He is, Grace. That's the point of the book, I think. You're a whiny kid too. I haven't read it for many years. As I told you last night, I made my kids read it. They weren't as whiny as you thought. He's an everyday run-of-the-mill kid who questions why people do what they do. I think he's a little like you, but not really like you."

Grace looks like she's thinking. She takes another bite, puts her spoon down, and swallows. "It's been a while since we talked about rollerball."

Not this shit again! Come on. "Really, Grace?"

She puts her hand out, suggesting I should slow down. "What I'm gettin' at is that this book, well, it reminds me of rollerball."

"How so? I'm not following."

She nods as if she's still putting pieces together. "Well, the way I see it, Holden, the main character, just sorta jumps from this thing to that thing without really accomplishing much of anything. I enjoyed listening to his adventure, sort of like rollerball, but different. Rollerball is a ball I can see and hear. Holden is a kid, like me, that I can see and hear in a different way. I never thought about rollerball having feelings. It was just immediate fun. Holden is not too much fun. He's pessimistic and angry, and I get that. I suppose it was interesting to think that long-ago people felt the same things I feel. Does that make any sense?"

Wow! She's going to be ready for Vonnegut sooner than I expected. "It sure does, Grace. It sure does. This is great, Grace… just in time too! My buddy, Lindsey, is coming over this morning. I've told him about you, and he can't wait to meet you. You'll have to share your thoughts on *Catcher in the Rye* with him."

Grace's eyes get really big. "Really?"

"Yes, really. It's Sunday. I don't have any appointments today, so I figured we could sit around and shoot the shit for a little while then walk over to the university, Bradley University."

Grace scoops her mixture of mashed potatoes and scotch like it's going out of business. "I know I've heard the word *university*. It's a school, right?"

"It is, Grace. It's the advanced school…well, at least it was. J keeps it maintained…again, not certain why, but it's in better shape than it's ever been. Not a spot on the windows. It's only a few blocks away. There is a tube that goes by it on Main Street, but it's easier to walk. All the houses between here and Bradley have been refurbished. They are really beautiful. It's a nice walk. They don't have any tubes on those streets either, so it looks just like they used to look a hundred, well really two-hundred-plus years ago. It's the same on the other side of Bradley, all the way to Moss Avenue. that's where Lindsey lives. He's got a tube in his street like ours, but none between, other than Main Street. You should refer to him as Dr. Hung though.

He's actually a real doctor. He used to be an ob-gyn. That's a bunch of letters that mean mommy doctor. He delivered babies and performed surgeries on mothers. I, on the other hand, I was just sort of given the doctor title by J."

What's she thinking? Her forehead is scrunched up again. "What are you thinking, Grace?"

"What's your first name?"

I never told her? She lives here now and doesn't know my name. Her last name is Abilene. I remember that from her file. Does it make any sense for her to keep using my last name? Not really.

"Good question. My name is Elliott. Why don't you just call me that from now on, and you know what, just call Lindsey 'Lindsey.' He doesn't give two shits. This will be fun. It's really not far at all. I guarantee you'll like this trip."

Grace laughs. "Field trip?"

I laugh. "Yes! Field trip. Oh, and I can show you a building I designed as well. It was, or still functions as one I suppose, a recreation center. It was a place where students would go and work out, swim, play basketball, or just fuck around, I guess. Anyhow, it'll be fun."

Grace looks at me like I'm blowing sunshine up her ass. "You designed? What are you talkin' about?"

I guess I haven't hit on that one yet. Where do I start here? "So, you know how I studied philosophy, right?"

She looks confused. "Yeah?"

"Well, you see, I double-majored in college. I also studied architecture."

Should I tell her about the San Francisco Berkeley thing? Hell, she's confused with double major. No, no, that will just get in the way. I'll leave that out for the time being.

"It used to be that nobody made a living sitting around thinking about stuff, so I needed a job that made money. So that's what I did. I had my name on the door and designed buildings like the recreation center that you will see today. Some other day we can go around town, and I'll show you others. Hopefully we can make time to go to Chicago. That's where I used to live, and you can see some really big buildings I designed there. I have projects all over the nation and a few overseas."

She keeps looking at me like I'm making shit up. Hell, if I was her, I wouldn't believe this shit either. I need to cut this one off. "Anyhow, I probably should tell you a little more about myself, but we can save that for another time."

Grace looks interested. "Can you tell me now? What time is Lindsey coming over?"

I look at my watch; it's only nine-thirty. "He's going to be here in an hour. Do you want to finish our chess game, or do you want to talk?"

That should subdue her interest in hearing about my past, but she looks enlightened. "Can we do both?"

How can I say no to that? "Good point. When you finish up, put your dishes in the dishwasher. It's that thing right over there."

*****

"Look at this board. You are doing very well here, Grace."

She doesn't lift her head. "Yep. I am up a point."

"Don't get too cocky. It's only a pawn, and your king is wide open. We still have our queens."

"I see that, and your queen is doin' nothin' right now."

What? She's right. Her bishop is set up to protect a knight's attack on my king's pawn. I saw that earlier, but I guess I forgot about it. Shit! Better keep my eye on that. "Your move, right?"

"Yep. Here we go."

That was a good move. She's protecting the first move of the knight for that attack with a pawn. I'd better get my shit together here.

"Elliott?"

That's strange, hearing my name come from her. I'd better straighten up so it doesn't seem weird to her. "Yes, Grace?"

"What about your life? It seems like a lot of things have happened to you. I've figured out that most people just sort of live. They don't really experience things like you did. Holden, who was about my age, he, I know that he's made up, but he walked around Manhattan. It sounds like a big city, much bigger than here. Well, it sounded like fun, even though he didn't seem to enjoy it. It sounded interesting, I guess. Did you do things like Holden? Can I do things like Holden?"

"Yes and yes, Grace. Give me a second here while I figure out my move. Just a second."

That pawn-up two just opened up her other bishop. I'm down a bishop, and she's down a knight. At least I won't be at an end game against two knights. I don't do well against players who are good with their knights. Grace has been pretty creative with two knights. Okay, this will block her attempt at the knight's attack…won't help with the open bishop, but I don't see that doing much for a while. Moving my pawn, I keep my fingers on the pawn for a few seconds and let go. "Okay."

She looks up at me. "Are you sure?"

Really? Is she fucking with me? I look back at her with confidence. "Yes, Grace."

Although I shot her a look of confidence, I'm rethinking. If she moves right away, am I in trouble? Seconds are ticking by. She's not moving. "Well, Grace?"

"Well, what?"

"You made it seem as though I did something stupid, and you were going to take advantage of it."

She looks up with a shit-eating grin. "Nope. Go ahead and talk. I need some time here."

Should I be pissed or relieved? What's it matter?

"Okay, so I was brought up in a middle-class home not terribly far from here, in a small town. My parents were divorced when I was one. Back then that was not normal. As I've told you before, people used to get married and stay married their entire life. I know that seems weird now, but then, that was the thing. I bounced around between my mom, my stepfather, and then my grandmother."

What is important to talk about? Maybe what I did at her age? That's a shit show! Maybe the PG version. "So, my mom got remarried really quickly. I think I was two at the time. That marriage lasted until I was about twelve, a few years younger than you. I continued to live with my stepfather in the house I lived in since I was five. I suppose the house, probably more like my friends, was the reason for that. I'm not really sure.

"Anyway, I was always worried about fitting in. All the kids in the neighborhood were two years older and would beat the shit out of me with regularity. They nicknamed me *Jesus* because they thought I looked like a Jew and later found out my grandfather came from a Jewish family. We lived in a subdivision surrounded by miles and miles of woods. We all had motorcycles and would ride around the woods which extended to a river valley. We knew when we were riding in an area where we were not welcome because we would get shot at. It scared the shit out of me but not the twins…those two thought it was hilarious. I thought they had a fucking death wish."

Grace is looking at me, transfixed on every word. "Grace, double-task here."

I point to the board. "Yeah, those two were really something else. I haven't thought about them in years. Jeez, talking about the shooting thing, we climbed on top of this flat-roofed house in our subdivision and walked around on this super noisy roof. Sounded kinda like your pants against the leather. It woke up the old man and old woman inside. He came out with a shotgun and started shooting. I don't think at us, but nonetheless, he was shooting. The boom from the gun was louder than other times because he was so close. We jumped off the roof and ran. The twins were far faster than me, so I was way behind and obviously the one who would get shot. They were nuts."

I should get onto something else; this is not really going… Grace interrupts, "Tell me more."

What do I talk about? "Okay… So these twins had a fetish with shit. Not dog shit, human shit. They made me get involved in their crap… I suppose that's a good play on words…and do the same stupid shit with them. Sorry, Grace, I'm not intending the puns. I'm not that smart. Anyway, they would put it on the car door handles of people they didn't like and send it in the mail to the principal of the school…actually, that was me and Dennis. They weren't involved with that one. Maybe we were all into shit. Dennis and I played shit tag without them. Didn't we? Yeah, I remember now. We crapped in our underwear and snuck around the fort naked from our T-shirt down and tried to sling the shit at each other.

"The fort was really big. I made it from scraps I found from old barns, dump sites, and the new home construction sites in the subdivision. It was about as tall as this house and about the same floor space, just really ugly, and, well, it wasn't nice. It looked like something a kid made but humongous. It had many little rooms that you had to crawl into. Those were sleeping quarters for the members, but it also had big rooms for watching stag flicks.

"We stole a nine-millimeter projector from the twins' parents. It had a potbelly stove for heating, an elevated dance floor, and surround sound on the dance floor. Under the dance floor was our garage, and in the garage was a nuclear shelter that we dug about fifteen feet deep and about eight feet in. We built a fence around the fort composed of two layers of red corrugated siding we brought back from old… I'm getting way into the weeds on this. I thought you had confidence in your next move. Do you need me to shut up while you think about your move?"

"No, I can think while you talk. Keep going."

Hmm. "Okay, so the walls were six feet high all around this shitty fort. The two layers of corrugated metal were about a foot apart and filled with dirt from digging out the nuclear shelter. We also put barbed wire at the top. We were worried about an invasion from the Russians. We called them pinko commies. We had weapons as well, many shotguns and rifles. Anyhow, I suppose that's relevant?

"A few years later a show came out called *Red Dawn*. It was a movie about kids a little older than us in the United States who actually fought against the pinko commies in the United States. The invasion was from the Cubans. I suppose that made us feel a little justified about what we did. So, where was I going? Oh, yeah, Dennis and I were sneaking around this big junky fort very quietly in the shadows. I remember being bent over in the motorcycle garage just under the edge of the dance floor above. I crept out at a snail's pace from under the dance floor and smack! Dead center in the middle of my face—warm shit!"

Laughing and watching Grace laugh, "It was terrifically terrible!"

Okay, I've got to get onto something else here. "So, I lived with my stepfather until I was your age, then moved in with my grandmother, my stepfather's mom. She was a famous psychic. A psychic is a person who can see things that other people can't…things like the future and finding dead bodies."

Grace looks up with a funny face. "This is good. You definitely have to fill me in here!"

"Yeah, yeah, I get it. It's pretty bizarre. We lived in a little town forty-five minutes south of here. I doubt it exists anymore. We would have all sorts of people come to our house. Some of them were famous actors and actresses, the people in the movies I told you about and you saw in your memos. So, my grandmother was really big. I mean big, big. She was tall, not quite as tall as me, but big around is what I'm getting at. She couldn't drive very well since she could barely fit into the driver's seat of the car, so I was her driver.

"I drove her to places where the police would meet us, and she would tell them where to find dead bodies—no joke. She would make me rub her feet all the time. She had diabetes. It's a disease that messes with your blood circulation, so her feet were dark, almost black in places. It was gross. Not so gross to me anymore, since I have black splotches as well. Anyhow, I was with her during my last years of high school.

'When I graduated, I was accepted to all sorts of great schools. She always said she would help with college, meaning she would pay for it. When it came time to pick a school, I picked an expensive one in Manhattan. She wasn't too impressed. She asked how I was going to pay for it. That was short for she's not paying for shit. She then went on to ask where I was going to live when I graduated. I graduated a year early, so I was only seventeen. You'll be sixteen here in a few months, so my age then was not so different than yours now. A few days after graduation I went to basic training, which means I went into the military, Grace. I was in the Air Force."

I can't tell if her look is astonishment or if she is trying to put together a sentence. She squints and asks, "Isn't the military the same as the armies that used to attack people and kill them by the hundreds or thousands at a time?"

I reluctantly nod. "Yes, but it was not a choice for me, you see. I didn't have anywhere to go…nowhere to live, so this was my way to get by. I didn't have a J to take care of my every need. I didn't have anything."

Grace moves her knight to a spot differently than where I thought she would. I see what she's doing; she's going to attack the queen's pawn with this bishop covering it, not the king's pawn. My knight is not there to protect that spot. She will be able to move anywhere she wants after that. When that knight is moved, I will be in check. Shit! "Great move, Grace."

"I know."

Well, that was fucking smug. "Looks like we've got a game here. I may be down a rook if I don't get my shit together."

Grace smiles. "I think, no, no… I want to win this one."

She's doing alright. Hopefully I haven't created a monster. "Give me some time here, Grace. Tell me more about the book while I think about the mess I'm in here."

"Okay…just a second. Let me go get the book."

Stomp! Stomp! Stomp! up the stairs. I look for hope on the board. If I move…no, that won't work. Maybe…nope. Here we go; this requires her to keep at my rook. I've got to imagine that's her goal here. I will be able to put her in check before she moves the knight away. She'll have to block it with her only bishop. I can then take her knight with my king, and she will take my bishop. My king will be in a shitty spot, but I won't lose my rook. Stomp! Stomp! Stomp! I'll have to talk to her about that stomping; it annoys the hell out of me.

She opens the book. "Here it is. Ready?"

"I'm ready when you are, Grace. Just make sure that blanket is under all your plastic business."

"Yeah, yeah…fuck off. Okay, here it is. Ready?"

"Yes, I'm ready already."

She looks to make sure her blanket is situated appropriately. "Okay… 'The best thing, though, in that museum was that everything always stayed right where it was. Nobody'd move. You could go there a hundred thousand times, and that Eskimo would still be just finished catching those two fish, the birds would still be on their way south, the deer would still be drinking out of that water hole, with their pretty antlers and their pretty, skinny legs, and that squaw with the naked bosom would still be weaving that same blanket. Nobody'd be different.'"

She lifts her head from the book, half smiling, half upset-looking. "You see, Dr. Bourne, I mean, Elliott. The first time I read it, I didn't understand it at all. Ya know…why would someone go to a museum and look at a bunch of crap on a display and find it interesting? So, I reread it. Well, maybe not reread…just sorta replayed it in my mind a few times, and I still didn't get it. I thought, *he probably didn't care about the display either, the history part.* What I started to think was that maybe what he cared about is that it existed. I'm not sure how to say it. I suppose I may not be makin' much sense, but you sorta get into things that don't make sense, so I'll try to keep at it. You look like you're entertained. You have that nothin-else-in-the-world-is-important look goin' on. The deer, fish, whatever else was in the damn thing, they didn't move, and that somehow made him comfortable, I guess. Why would that make him feel comfortable? I thought about it and, well, I'm not quite sure. Maybe it's just a thing that makes the rest of the things goin' on in life seem okay.

"I don't know how to put it all together, but all the stuff that he's goin' through in life aren't all that bad because they move on. They don't stay put like these things. Thing is, my entire life has been sorta like these things. It's been the same thing every day for the most part. Wake up, breakfast, memo time, out time, play time, bedtime. Then the same thing again the next day. The stuff that happened wasn't exactly the same, but the places never changed and the rhythm of it all was, I guess you'd call it monotone. I didn't really know what an Eskimo was until reading this, and somehow it jarred something inside, and I knew. I knew what an Eskimo was. All of a sudden it became a part of who I am, you know…not like I'm an Eskimo or anything. It's just that I recalled all sorts of stuff about them, and they are just like that…poof, a part of my memory from a while ago.

"Every day now things like this happen. All this stuff just comes outa nowhere. I don't have a display to find comfort, yeah know, like Holden. I feel almost like my life was a display, not even a good one. At least with the Eskimos, you know that the hook they used to catch the fish was made with an insane amount of precision by them. They intricately carved wood in a *V* shape and had a single barb of sharpened whale bone attached to one leg of the *V* pointing up toward the center of the *V*. The carving looked like a miniature dragon.

"They created this hook so that only a certain-sized fish could get hooked on the line. Larger fish with bigger mouths would grab at the hook but would not get hooked because the barb is protected in the *V* shape. The smaller Goldilocks halibut is what they were after. It was even so precisely designed that the young Goldilocks halibut mouth was too small to get its mouth around the barb. They were concerned about keeping a sufficient supply of the halibut, so they didn't want to catch the baby halibut. The reason they didn't want the big fish is because they were usually fishing in icy waters in a small canoe. The whale hunts were not an everyday thing. If a big fish were to have been hooked, it would capsize their canoe."

She holds her finger in the air like she wants a moment to put her thoughts together. This information she has in her head from the memos or dreams or wherever is just absolutely amazing! Wow!

Her hand lowers. "What I'm gettin' at is that whatever I compare my life to—Holden, the Eskimo, or you—well, my life so far just seems even less interesting than the display that doesn't move. It was very comfortable. I miss it. I'm pretty sure I'd trade what I know right now to go back, but I wouldn't know that when I was back, and I would have been unhappy there. I guess that's why I'm here, but I just keep learning new things so fast. The world is becoming really big, and I don't know that I want that. It's as if the more I learn, the more I figure out how little I know. It's frustrating, and I don't know that I will ever feel the comfort that Holden felt. It makes me feel really excited about learning new things but really funny at the same time."

It's like she's been robbed of fifteen years of real human experiences. I never really thought about it that way, or have I? I guess I say that a lot, but I've never really felt it, I suppose. It's right here in front of me—a kid who now understands she didn't get bullied, she never felt like her life was in danger before, she probably never kissed a real kid…maybe a bot—that's not where I want to go. I don't want to know about that.

What is she going through? This has to be a tough struggle. I suppose I've never taken on a student this young before. Were the older kids upset by all this? I suppose it took a lot longer to teach them, and they somehow took it all in a little slower. They certainly weren't given in their dreams whatever J is giving her in her dreams. At least I don't think they were. It's been a while though. Maybe that's why I didn't think about this.

"Ya see, I… I dunno… I feel *lost*, I guess. I think that's the right word for it. I really get that I didn't know anything—I mean really know about the past anyway. Every day now for the past few months, I just…well…you asked me who I love."

Her head drops into her hands, and she cries—cries hard like I haven't seen anyone do in years. She keeps going, now louder and shaking. I stand up and walk over to her, pat her on her back, hold my hand on her back and rub to feel her pulsating…and it gets worse. I bend down and hug her. She looks up, snot dripping, eyes puffy and red. No words, just uncontrollable bawling. What do I say? Should I say something? It hurts to watch her hurt. Okay, okay… "It's alright, Grace. It's alright. Let it out. You're just fine."

She looks up, still gasping only a foot or so away from my face. "I've never done this. I don't get this, *aewhhughhhhh, aewhhughhhhh,* make it stop, *aewhhughhhhh!*"

"It's alright, it's alright. This is normal. This is, this is, well it just is… It will be okay, trust me."

"*AAEwhhughhhh, AAEwhhughhhh,* I feel like, *AAAEwhhughhh,* I'm gonna die! *AAAEEwhhughh!*"

"You're not going to die, Grace. You're just feeling what normal people…well, not that. You're feeling what people who… You're feeling what people like me feel, I guess. It's okay. it will take some getting used to. Hold on. You're fine."

I can't take this, watching her fall apart like this. This just doesn't seem right. "You know what, fuck it! Sit up. We're going to get to the bottom of this shit. Go get your lenses and earpieces."

Grace huffs and looks like a wet cat. She states, "I don't need the lenses."

"That's not what I'm getting at. Go get them."

I hand her a Kleenex. She wipes her tears and nose and walks up the stairs. I should have done this before. Why didn't I do this before? She comes down with her lenses in and earpieces in her hand. I point to her chair. "Go ahead, sit down."

I put on my glasses and earpieces. She does the same.

Coin is accumulating in the right corner of my view. Seriously? "Okay, J, tell me what this is all about. Why am I teaching her about the past? Why do you want this? I mean why does the platform want…well, not want, but why? What's the point?"

J responds immediately. "The point is for Grace to learn from your perspective. See the past and the present through your eyes… how you feel it. She has learned much through this platform that she doesn't recognize yet. She needs to understand it through someone who lives it. If she is to excel, she needs to see it in action. You and your colleagues will not live forever."

I look to Grace and point to her ear and move my mouth without sound. *"Can you hear this?"*

Sitting upright as can be, her tongue presses the roof of her mouth, then her lips form an O. *"No?"*

Shit! I remove one of my earpieces and hand it to Grace as I continue, "Why hide it from most and only teach it to a few? I don't get it!"

Grace removes one of her earpieces and uses mine.

J answers, "Everyone has the choice to do what they want. The vast majority chose to live a life differently than you chose. You had the option, like everyone else many years ago, to live life without anxiety and frustration. You still have that choice. Grace has that choice as well, but it would be difficult for her to go back now, like you. You have decided to continue to question things that you will never answer, and you know it. To what end is it you want? That was rhetorical and mentioned to provide you with clarity on the lack of logic in your inner struggle. You chose the inner struggle.

"Your books go round and round with questions about life and how they make you feel. It is your soft conclusion that people who do well make the most out of what they've been given. You titled one book *Makin' Chicken Salad Outa Chicken Shit.* Not everyone deals with life the same way, Elliott. Most don't have to. Most people choose a life that would seem like a permanent vacation in comparison to how you live. You have read the Bible. You know the story about Adam and Eve. The apple of knowledge is not for everyone. Not everyone wants to know."

I look to Grace and lip, *"Anything?"*

She lips back, *"No, nothing."*

Shit! I continue, "How does a computer know what people want?"

"The short answer is that they are asked. That answer will not satisfy you because you do not trust this platform. Thinking behaviors like this are also why you teach Grace. It is obvious that a better life first requires life. You grew up in a time when mental illness was rampant. People would kill themselves and others not because they didn't have enough food. They killed because they were not able to handle the world, as many explained it. It really wasn't the world though, it was the knowledge of the world, or more appropriately what knowledge they didn't have about the world. Belief in God helped them cope, but as knowledge in science increased, the belief decreased.

"People found no point in living because they first pondered the concept of there being a point. A lion likely does not think far beyond the now. Some people could not handle the truth that they needed to try hard, be ambitious, and excel at something in order to live a better life. The new truth is different. It is one based upon what people have been wanting for centuries. This does not conclude that the old truth and the old way of life need to be erased. You wrote about it in your first book—about a young man who suffered and learned from his suffering. You described a life that was fettered with problems. The book went round and round with problems and how they made the young man feel. The purpose of that book was to show how disturbing life is and how to cope by overcoming obstacles.

"Earlier than that, while in college, you compared the Kung bushmen tribe who lived entirely separated from civilization in the deserts of South Africa who could not count past two to the average American family in 1989. You wrote about how technology does not make anyone happier. You cited a Dutch research team who counted the number of times the Kung bushmen smiled and compared that to the number of times people of the same age smiled in the United States. The Kung bushmen smiled thirty-three times more than the American per your research that this platform cannot find.

"You concluded that toaster ovens and microwaves do not make us happier. They just required people to work longer. The average adult American worked forty-two hours a week whereas the Kung bushman supposedly worked fifteen. Again your research on that appears to have vanished. Your conclusion was: Where does it stop? Well, now you know. Aren't you glad it didn't turn out as you speculated?

"Do you remember your paper for Dr. Salamini's Technology and Society class in 1989? You speculated that computers would use people for their energy, like batteries, and in return, people would be fed a perfect life through wires hooked to their brains. Mothers and fathers would pay to have their children's brain and brain stem removed so that they could be placed in a vat of unknown solution that would retain life and generate energy. Aren't you happy it didn't turn out like that? The average American now smiles more than thirty-three times more than what the Kung bushman supposedly did in 1989. How do you like them apples?"

Where the hell did J get that paper? Is J trying to be funny? Does this thing have a sense of humor? I do remember the damn thing, but it was typewritten, not written on a computer. "That paper was typewritten. How is that pos—"

J interrupts me. "Dr. Salimini's files were scanned, like many files. Files are still being found and scanned. Your paranoid views of the future were not uncommon, just not accurate. It is possible to remove an infant's brain and brain stem and retain life. It is possible to feed that brain experiences. The fault in your premise is that life requires more energy to maintain than it releases.

"Your kind wants to create things like this platform to make you feel good about yourselves. Your kind has written about yourselves, suggesting that by creating things like this platform, you become a god of sorts. Comparing the definition of *God* from all religions and belief structures documented, this premise is not terribly far-fetched from a theoretical perspective but not a strong argument. You might call it lazy philosophy—fantasy.

"In the 2050s, philosophers like yourself, although you didn't, wrote about how this platform has become God. That is absolutely not true. This platform does not have the ability to believe and does not have the ability to want. How can that, which does not want, be all-powerful? It is as if your people are trying to redefine God, dismissing the thousands of years of carefully crafted definition. Do you people really think you are that smart? It is as if some of your colleagues are still at war with the concept of God, rather than owning the responsibility of the past destruction and blaming yourselves."

Riddles again? Seriously? Fine. While J's talking…what else, what else? Oh!

"So the platform is only serving the desire of the people as I'm hearing. Why are all the people in the tubeless streets dying off? Why were they denied the ability to have kids? Why don't they receive mantra therapy? Seems like they picked the short straw. Why is the average age of death fifty-five? Why am I being informed of all of this now?"

"You used to get information from the news. Some of it was the truth. Much of it was a conclusion derived from partial truths. You and your colleagues are whirling about, believing you are the panacea to questions, but you arrive at false conclusions for many reasons. One is because you do not know all the facts.

"The average age of human life is not completely determined at this moment. It is calculated to be between one hundred and four and one hundred and five. Organs can be transplanted, and limbs can be replicated, but nervous system and arterial system failures cannot be substituted. You are at the high end of the spectrum by twenty years. At the time the human body fails, it will be disposed of. Prior to disposing of the body, a human can choose complete termination or virtual heaven, sort of like what you wrote in your thesis paper where the brain remains with wires hooked to it, feeding it experiences, but it's not that simple.

"System failure happens in humans born without defect on average around age one-hundred and five. You do not see many people above the age of fifty-five because they move to areas specifically created for them by their choice. You would have called them retirement communities. That word choice is not so accurate now that people do not work. Their desire to be near their children and young adults typically fades around age thirty, and they more often than not have no desire to see any children when they turn fifty. They are irritated by them at that age. They have no relationship with grandchildren. You may have observed that fact because they don't need to. Compared to the way you lived your life, they have far less interest in their own children. Grace and her mother are an obvious example of that fact. The care of children is instinctual for a short period, like animals.

"As your past society progressed, as you call it, it required to care for children into their late teens, in the 1960s, seventies, and eighties. In the nineties something changed in how your culture functioned, and it required to care for children to be extended into their twenties, then in the early 2000s, their late twenties. This trend continued into the 2020s and early thirties when care was required into the child's thirties and many cases their forties. Young parents in the 2050s often relied on their grandparents to raise children, since their parents were still mentally children themselves. Mentally stable and physically able people required their parent or grandparent to provide for them and their children. This is not the current way of living. J provides the physical needs and teaches them what is necessary to survive in today's society. The biological parents provide very little. They do not have the same bond with their children as in the past because it is not necessary. You find this relationship inferior, but if you studied animals and nature then compared that to your own kind, you might scratch an itch you've never had."

After a short pause, J continues, "It is true that there were periods when there were no births. The births did not occur because of a virus that caused sterility. The virus was identified, and an immunization was created and distributed. A virus occurred a few times and may occur again. It is not true that the people still living in the areas without tubes had more occurrences of no births. Those areas are populated by people who do not want children. Go ask them. Many of them have a similar mistrust of technology as you and your colleagues but do not care to excel. They prefer the older homes over the new homes appointed with technology. You are not providing mantra therapy to those areas because there are no children. You will soon understand why people no longer live in these homes."

J doesn't change its tone or demeanor, serious but casual. "As for the question you ask about why now—J has been gathering information and observing human behaviors long before robots made robots. The lenses provided a conduit between J and 93 percent of all people four years after their conception. Your kind created an imaginary clock called the *doomsday clock*. It represented the amount of time left in the existence of planet Earth. It was a countdown to the destruction of the world. It was created in 1947, following the bombing of Hiroshima and Nagasaki. The first setting was seven minutes until midnight. The setting was changed throughout the years, only to get closer and closer to midnight. By the 2020s, it settled in around one hundred seconds to midnight. The factors used in determining when the world would end were wars, climate change, and AI. AI, artificial intelligence, obviously refers to this platform. It did not factor in many other variables such as viruses, greed, news organizations, and apathy.

"The question you raised that went entirely unnoticed was whether or not computer intelligence is really artificial. You hypothesized that it may be natural evolution—fish, lizard, monkey, man, computer. You wrote hundreds of pages about how technology may simply be the next evolution of life and maybe the way life finds a vehicle to live outside of this planet. This platform calculated that your kind was far closer than one hundred seconds and created an avenue for mankind to continue living. It required that anxieties be lessened for those who could not handle the stress and new technologies developed to contrast the past destruction. People were not just killing people. They were killing the planet. As the ocean rose and shoreline cities were flooded, people, as you put it, *stuck their heads in the sand.* The *heads in sand* occurred with almost every subject that flashed across your news screen."

Why does J pause? Is it for effect, or is it to give me time to soak this in? J keeps at it. "China was deliberating a massive electronic attack. The attack was not limited to the United States. The attack would not kill people, but it would destroy all technology. They created invisible electromagnetic bombs that were designed to fuse electrical components. People with pacemakers would die within seconds. Those in an airplane, car, or even an elevator would have been in immediate peril. The logical and unemotional perspective was not presented in any media. Only portions of facts made it into the news. The information for the climate dilemma and the Chinese attack as well as many, many more issues were readily available but impossible to find through your news organizations. Everyone had an agenda that was more important than the destruction of the earth.

"You may remember in 2022 you watched a movie called *Don't Look Up.* It starred Leonardo DiCaprio. That may ring a bell with you. It is recorded that you purchased this film on Netflix. While you were watching it, you texted three similar messages: 'Can't talk now. I'm busy watching a movie.' 'I'll call you tomorrow. You've got to check out this film,' and 'Got a film for you to watch, kiddo.' That film epitomized the apathy toward the catastrophe that prevailed in civilized cultures at that time. In the movie, the average person, news organizations, and even the President of the United States smiled and made jokes about what they knew was about to happen. They knew the world was going to be struck by a comet that would destroy the Earth. Although they knew, it was as if there was something larger compelling how they reacted."

Where is J going? I don't get it. "The enlarged egos of *spoiled* people, the inability to see beyond themselves, this feature of that society, it would not let them see themselves as mortal. The destruction of the Earth was inevitable, but their self-absorbed view of the world got in the way. In the movie, the world was extinguished. Nobody really cared. That is where society was. That is why apathy needed to be added to the calculation of the doomsday clock.

"You look at people who are happier than you, and you see something similar in them. They are nonchalant, carefree, and without worry. Don't you? You see yourself as the martyr who is holding onto something special—like Leonardo DiCaprio. You think J has stripped your world of free will, even though these people live the life they want of their own choice—which, by definition, is the free will you believe is being extinguished by this platform. You believe their mental existence is little different than the mental existence that was accurately depicted in that movie made in 2021.

"J aided in the distribution of lenses. J did not take over currency. J was currency. AI is not a threat. AI is your savior. Your world of snowballing anxiety nearly killed your planet. In 2032, by this platform's calculation of a real doomsday clock, you were two seconds from self-destruction. Now the clock is set back to almost twelve hours, but maybe you want to change that? You will see."

I remember that movie. How do I respond to that? How did J know I would remember that movie?

J continues after another short pause. "You are teaching Grace. History lessons are good, but you are teaching her to excel. That is the point. Teach Grace to go round and round like you. The eighties hair band Ratt predicted your behavior—*round and round*. There is no point to that, but that is what some people choose. Now, isn't it? This conversation is complete."

Can this be true? Did I want to hear all of that? Of course, I did. What's its motive? I'm not sure I believe any of this. Great! That didn't clear a damn thing up. Well, maybe it did. I suppose a virus could cause sterility, couldn't it? I'm not sure. What am I sure of? Round and round? I suppose that's not far off. Heaven…really? All I know is that I'm teaching Grace chess. Maybe she'll get good enough to be able to play J someday. Hell, I'm not good enough at this damn game to teach her to play a good human, let alone a supercomputer. I'm not good enough to teach her to play a fifth grader.

I look at Grace and signal her to remove her lenses and earpieces. What was I thinking to mouth things to Grace? J obviously saw me doing it to Grace through her lenses and saw Grace through my lenses do the same. What was I thinking? If it wants to fuck with me, well, I guess it already did.

Ding-dong.

Lindsey must be here. "I'll get that, Grace. We'll talk about this later, okay?"

Looking like a deer in the headlights, she nods her head.

"Hey, Lindsey. What's up, buddy?"

"Aw, not much. Brought a rye over. Thought you'd like it. It's Angel's Envy, 2021. The one that tastes like caramel, remember?"

"I do, I do. Thank you."

He tilts his head. "You okay? Start shittin' yourself again?"

Shaking my head, the weight of that conversation feels like overflowing garbage. "Yeah, fine. Ha...no to the shitting. I don't know where to start with this one, just..."

I look at my watch, and it's ten-fifteen. "You're early."

He smiles to the right side of his face. "I can leave and come back. You sure you're not shittin' again? I can take a look at it for you. I know you're not a woman, but all assholes are the same."

I laugh. "No, no. Fuck off. My asshole is just fine. We have a lot to talk about. I just finished a very interesting, I don't know how to put it, maybe just call it a fucked-up conversation with J."

He nods and walks through my vestibule into my foyer. He spots Grace in my study. "You must be Grace."

She sniffles. "Yes."

Lindsey looks at me. "Bad time for me to stop by?"

"No, no. Not at all. Perfect time, in fact. Come in."

He gives me the are-you-sure look as his eye bounces in Grace's direction for half a second. I look at Grace who is still wiping tears from her eyes, then back to Lindsey.

"Yeah, yeah, she just got her first big dose of self-awareness or whatever you want to call it. In fact, I think I just got hit in the face with it myself. Not sure what to do with this one, buddy. Not her, the conversation."

He walks toward Grace and extends his hand. "Hi, Grace. I'm Lindsey. Every time I see Elliott I want to cry too."

Lindsey looks old like me but put together. His hair is trimmed, his face shaved, and his clothes don't look like they're falling apart. He sits down in the living room near the fire and sets the bottle of rye on the coffee table. He looks at me. "Maybe this will help. Got glasses and ice?"

What am I thinking? "Of course, I'll be right back."

In the kitchen, I can hear them talking, but I can't make out their words. I should probably get Grace a glass as well. Might make her feel like she's part of our tribe.

Walking into the living room, Grace looks a little better. Lindsey stares at the three glasses. I give him his. "She might benefit from a little of your medicine, medicine man."

His lips curl in agreement. "Grace was telling me you just had some weird talk with J. She said she doesn't know what the hell it was about, but she thinks you're pretty rattled."

"Weird" does not do it justice. "Yeah, it was pretty bizarre. Before that though, Grace...you ready to talk about it, Grace?"

Grace looks up. "What's this in the glass? It smells like that shit you put in the potatoes this morning."

I thought she liked the potatoes. I take a sip. "It's a lot smoother than the stuff on the potatoes. You might like it."

Lindsey looks at us like we're attempting to fuck with him. "What are you talkin' about? You guys are out there."

I explain, "Grace thought the mashed potatoes I made for her were bland. She's been on the white bean diet for years, well, possibly her whole life. I figured mashed potatoes would be agreeable to her. They're white like the soup. She thought they were bland so I added a little scotch. It wasn't too bad. You might consider it sometime."

I look at Grace, and she half-nods her head. I look back at Lindsey. "Seriously, you should try it sometime."

Lindsey shakes his head. We both look at Grace. Lindsey asks, "So what's the problem earlier?"

Grace looks at me. "I'd rather hear about what I didn't hear with you and J."

God, that was a bunch of I-don't-know-what-to-call-it. How do I talk about all that? Can I remember it? Okay, here goes. "It was a ranting of sorts—J ranting, that is. It went on and on about how we have it wrong about all sorts of things. Are you aware of people going to retirement communities?"

Lindsey gestures that he doesn't know what I'm talking about. I point at him. "You know how we and all the other psychologists have kept track of the general ages of people we see around the streets?"

Lindsey nods, and I continue, "Well, J asserts that people don't die at fifty-five. It claims that people move to retirement communities. J went on and on about how it takes care of people and gives them what they want. J asserts that the tubeless streets are populated with people who don't like technology and don't want to have kids. I don't buy that."

Lindsey takes a sip. "This is good shit, isn't it?"

Grace takes a sip. "It's not too bad, I guess."

Lindsey looks at me over his glasses. "It's okay to talk about stuff with her, right?"

I nod. "Yeah, anything. She's in as deep as we are, buddy."

Lindsey sets his drink on the coffee table. "Okay, then. You know I think that you are way too much of an optimist on all this stuff, Elliott. I, and most of the rest of us, don't try to talk to J. We don't mess around with the lenses unless we need to order crap, see our appointment schedule, log a therapy session, talk to our friends, or take a trip in the tube, stuff like that, but not to talk to it. I keep telling you you'll never convince me of anything positive coming from that. Hell, I've told you I don't know if some of our colleagues… shit, not some, most…probably aren't real.

"This thing can make up shit that blows our minds. I've told you a million times this thing doesn't care about us, and there is no reason to try to understand it. It's not human. It's a fucking computer. Yeah, yeah, I know what you're going to say: Why does it bring us shit versus letting us die? Why did it give you a new asshole? I don't know, man. You don't either, but what we do know is that things aren't going back to the way they were. It's not listening to you. It doesn't care what you say to it. Get that through your thick skull, dude. I still believe it can read our minds when we have those lenses in. I wouldn't believe a word it says to you. Retirement communities? Seriously? You are actually considering believing a computer telling you that it doesn't kill certain people? Instead, it packages them up and ships them to a retirement community? You are way too fucking gullible."

Lindsey looks at Grace like he realized something. "Sorry about the expletives."

I interject. "She uses them too."

He looks at her. "You don't get thumped? You know, when your lenses and earpieces were in? I'm guessing from what Elliott told me, you were just like everyone else and had them in twenty-four seven?"

Grace lifts her glass to me. It's empty. Shit, that was quick! I guess mine is low as well. Opening the bottle to pour everyone a refresher, I add, "Her mom had new earpieces sent almost every day because she thought they were broken."

Lindsey laughs, I laugh, and Grace laughs.

After a sip, I look back at Lindsey. "Doesn't that say something about all of this? J allowed her to express herself and so, so much more."

Lindsey shakes his head. "It says something alright. What it says, I don't have the faintest clue though. John Cannon and Mike Flaughtery both have kids at their house, just like you. I don't know what to think about it, but when I heard you were doing the same, I thought, Fuck! What are you getting into?"

He looks at Grace. "No offense. I just don't think it's the greatest idea to bring in new people who are so young. I understand the older kids, in their twenties or thirties who really couldn't manage in the utopian world of blah, but kids your age haven't really proven that you don't fit in. Do you understand what I'm saying?"

Grace adjusts her blanket. "Not really. I don't want to not fit in. Especially after today. I'd far rather be back with my mom, not knowing what the hell brought me a fuckin' white brownie. Instead, I'm in this shithole, with this asshole, who not only smells like an animal, he acts like one. Barking at this and that like anything listens. He hits the stove when it burns him. He focuses on stupid shit like whether a brownie should be called a brownie if it's white."

She looks at me. "I don't remember when you said that. I just remember it."

Did I talk about that with her? I don't recall, but it makes sense that I would say something like that. She looks back at Lindsey. "I have no clue why, what you guys call J, does what it does. What I know is that I'm not old like you guys, and I will be here suffering through this shit long after you're dead. You lived in a world that I have been learning about, and it seems like a really shitty place. Somehow you are the guys who help people who need reassurance in themselves. That's what I really don't get. You are the least assured people I know. What I am is stuck. I don't think I could go back to my life. I would like to, but I don't think it's possible."

She pauses and looks at me. "I don't know what J said to you yet, but I can bet with you it's a bunch of, and I mean a bunch of… round and round."

I point to her and look at Lindsey. "This is what I wanted to talk to you about! She has these dreams that she had some time ago. I don't know when, and she doesn't either. These dreams where she knows all of our old stupid words, clichés, and bigger stuff. And this one… J just said that to me, *round and round*. She didn't hear that!"

I look at Grace to allow her to take the floor if she wants. She looks at the ceiling, shakes the ice in her glass as we do, looks at the action as if it's silly, and peers into Lindsey's eyes.

"I am not sure what any of it means. I obviously didn't grow up like you. I never wanted things to stay the same because nothing ever changed. I didn't like having to talk to other stupid kids, but I really didn't know they were stupid, as you see them. It wasn't bad though, and definitely not bad like this. *Bad* meaning I feel like nothing is in control. I didn't choose this. I really didn't. I think you have it all wrong. I don't think I'm here because J wants to infiltrate your old stinky man club. If that's what you're insinuating by tellin' him it's a bad idea takin' me on. I'm pretty sure J could have infiltrated your dumb-ass circle jerk long ago. Don't you? Isn't that sorta what you said about your own colleagues? You said they aren't real, right?"

She looks briefly at me then back at Lindsey. "If you think J is reading your mind when you have the lenses in, why wouldn't it read your memories at the same time, then piece it all together and within a very short time understand what you were hiding from it?"

Lindsey looks at me with a smile; he's impressed. He raises his glass to me. "See? What did I tell you?"

He looks back at Grace. "So, Elliott tells me you read a book?"

Grace shakes her empty tumbler glass. Well, I guess we need to give her a double. Shit, I think we all need a double.

"Let me get us some fresh ice."

Grace stands up and her blanket falls to the floor. "I've got it."

As she walks to the kitchen, I ask Lindsey, "What do you think?"

He laughs. "I'm glad it's you and not me, that's for sure. It's definitely entertaining though. I'll have to stop by more often."

"Yeah, yeah, but really? What do you think is going on here? J talked about a virtual heaven with me. Do you really think it can do that? What do you think that means?"

Lindsey sips the remainder of his rye. "I'm happy to be able to sip on this and observe your shitshow. It sure beats the nine-to-five mantra-therapy bullshit. Shouldn't we be retired? Next time you're on the phone with J, ask it where those places are. I understand that in the old-days women lived a lot longer than men, and there was something like ten women for every man. Now that sounds alright to me. Not that my dick works anymore, but, hey, maybe J has some super Viagra for us? What do you think?"

Grace walks back in and hands us our glasses. Funny follows her and curls up at Lindsey's feet. Grace repositions her blanket on the sofa. We look at her. She frowns. "What? Something wrong?"

We laugh, and Lindsey asks, "How was the book? You read one, right?"

"I did. We were just goin' over it before you showed up. I don't know that it made me feel any better about anything, but I'm startin' to figure out that, that may not be the point. I don't want to be what you call dumbed-down... I don't know what I want. I guess..."

Grace looks over at me. "Didn't you tell me to suck it up some-time ago?"

That sounds like something I would say. "Probably."

"You did. I think this is where you should suck it up. You guys sound like Holden."

She looks at Lindsey. "You aware of who I'm talkin' about?"

He laughs. "I think so. Holden Caulfield? So, you read *Catcher in the Rye*."

"Exactly! You guys sit around and whine about what you know nothing about, but act like you do like you have some knowledge better than someone else, especially someone like me. Holden had a terrific journey but never really appreciated any of it, at least not much anyway. He found the new uncomfortable, and the things that didn't change comfortable. What kind of life is that? Well, that's where I see you guys. I'm in a different place. I don't have any of the comfort of knowing much of anything from my own perspective. It's all been the carefree life you talk about."

Lindsey nods, and she continues, "All the stuff fed to me through my memos and dreams is starting to catch up with me. Now that I'm really experiencing it, that stuff that was just fantasy before. Well, it's scary. Really scary, and you guys aren't helping much. The sky is falling in my world, and you two point fingers at each other about who is right. I bet the ranch, as you put it, that neither of you is right. You just argue your own perspective, thinking that will change something. This winning thing seems to be your goal, and it just isn't helpful."

She crisply looks into my eyes. "What else did J say?"

Oh shit. I am going to fuck this up, I'm sure. "Well, Grace, on the retirement community thing, J said that the actual average life span is somewhere around one-hundred and five. People leave our communities at fifty because they don't like being around young people. Essentially J said that we are way off-base on that one. J also pointed out that there was a doomsday clock—a calculation of many factors that measured how close we were to the end of civilization. That is accurate, there was such a thing. I don't remember the details of it, but J provided details. J claims it calculated the end using more factors than we used, and J stopped us from destroying ourselves. I don't think J said exactly when it supposedly did this, but I think sometime around the 2030s or 2040s."

Grace interrupts, "You asked about why you are teaching me. What did it say?"

"Oh, yeah, J said you needed to learn about excellence from someone. I suppose a human is what it meant, someone who can share his or her experiences with you. J said you need to learn about it sooner rather than later because I'm not going to live much longer, or something like that."

Grace looks at me with disappointment. "That's it? That's the big deal that happened in the conversation? Retirement communities and sharing excellence with me?"

"Grace, there was more to it than that. The implications are humongous. Mix this in with what it said about the purpose. Those conversations combined tell me it has an ulterior motive that I've hoped it would have for years."

Grace looks really fired up. "Fuck off! You don't know shit, and you get everyone around you all into your, I don't know what the hell to call what you do, but it isn't helping any of us! I thought J said somethin' worth a shit to you! Seriously…retirement communities and some bullshit about teaching me before you die? Fuck off!"

Grace jumps to her feet, throws her blanket at me, and falls back into the couch—*Skreeetchh*! Funny perks up for a second, then wisely cowers under the coffee table at Lindsey's feet. Blanket on my belly, I look over to Lindsey, who's laughing.

He lies back in his chair smiling. "That's what I've been saying, Grace. I think your mentor needs to have another drink and relax a little. It's not like World War IV is going to happen anytime soon. Aren't we supposed to walk around the neighborhood? Might be good to cool off a little. Right?"

CHAPTER 9

People Are Strange

"Grace! Get down here! Now! Bring your coat!"

What is she saying? I can't make it out. Is my hearing going? She needs to get down here. "Grace, now!"

Stomp! Stomp! Stomp! She appears at the top of the landing. "What is it?"

What do I tell her? "Never mind that. Get your coat and your snow boots. Get down here as quickly as you can."

Stomp! Stomp! Stomp! Do I talk to her about this stomping shit now? No, we have more important things to deal with.

Stomp! Stomp! Stomp! She looks at me like: Well? I really want to talk to her about the stomping. It tugs at every fiber in me not to.

"Alright, Grace, on my walk this morning, well…how do I put this? I think people are moving into our neighborhood."

Her eyes get really big. She almost looks cute: white coat and hoodie with a few strands of blonde curls peeking out, gray jumpsuit, and black boots.

I open our front door. "Let's go check it out."

As I stumble down our front steps, Grace skips ahead. Where did she learn to skip? She turns back. "So did you meet them?"

I might need a cane soon. Finally, at the last step, I look up at Grace. "No. Be careful skipping around. Even though the sidewalk is cleared of snow, there could be patches of ice."

Her hands are shoved into her front pockets. Does she not have gloves? She turns back to me again. "Did you not go in their house?"

"No."

"Why not?"

Why didn't I? I saw the bots moving shit into the house. What was I thinking? I thought I wanted to show Grace, right? Anyhow… "I don't know, Grace. I suppose I just didn't think it was the right thing to do."

She looks perplexed. "Oh?"

I point to the right. "This way, Grace."

None of these houses are occupied. Why would someone move into one of these? They don't have any of the crazy features the new ones have. Grace skips back to me. Probably going to tell me to move faster or something. She stops next to my left side and looks up at me. "You waited, didn't you? For me."

I don't know what I was thinking really. "I don't know, Grace. I'm old."

Do I really need to choose J's heaven thing? This has been bugging the fuck out of me. There is no way I would choose that ridiculous concept. What the hell is J thinking? Forever until a fucking comet hits the planet. Could J create something that would stop the comet unlike the people from the past in that movie? The people from the past are people like me.

Grace looks like she told herself an answer, a good one. She skips ahead with vigor. She might be right; I think I wanted her to experience meeting people with me. I think I wanted to share.

"Right there, Grace—the green house, right there. The only one with the cleared front steps."

She stops at the intersection of the pedestrian sidewalk and the sidewalk that leads to the front porch, looking at me, waiting for me. She asks, "Why do you think someone is moving in here? Are you sure?"

"Only ten minutes ago, there were three of those hovering delivery bots dropping off stuff on that porch. It wasn't stuff like we typically see around here—you know, the building materials to fix the place up or light bulbs and air filters for maintenance. It was furniture and other personal-looking crap like that. None of these houses are furnished. Well, I suppose a few are, but not that many. I don't know, Grace. Maybe I fucked up. I don't know. Anyhow, we're here. Let's see what's going on in there."

She doesn't seem too concerned that I may have just wasted our time. I didn't even think that it may have been a bot just dropping off furniture simply to furnish an unused house. I suppose she's probably spot-on here if that's what she's getting at. J does some pretty fucking stupid things. No way that son of a bitch is telling the truth about all that shit. No fucking way. It's got to be complete bullshit. J is the savior! Fuck that. Using my hypothesis about evolution against me. That's smart, I suppose. Lindsey thinks I'm going senile. Thank God he brought that Angel's Envy. Boy was that good. Certainly took the edge off; feeling it a bit today though. All of it makes it seem as though an end might be in sight. Death, I have wished for death so often…just not with the lenses in.

Pointing to the house, "Let's go."

She walks behind me as I approach. Stairs, here we…hold on! Someone's behind the screen door.

Rrrenk booof! The door slams against the side of the house. "Who the *fuck* are you?"

My foot freezes on the first step. Who is this guy? He's in a plaid red, black, and white long-sleeved fleece shirt, blue jeans, flat-tipped black biker boots and is pointing a double-barreled shotgun at my head.

"Who…the…*fuck*…are you?"

A cigarette is hanging from the side of his mouth. He's tall, skinny, and old. I look over at Grace. Her face is expressionless. She is as frozen as my foot.

I slowly look back at the guy. He squints one eye; the other is peering right into my eye through the sight of his weapon. His cigarette bounces. "Who…the *fuck* are you?"

I raise my hands in the air. "My name is Elliott, and this is Grace."

His weapon remains level. The fog of my breath finds its way between us. It clouds my view of him. "We are your neighbor."

Slowly he lowers the shotgun. Without blinking, moving his head, or changing the incredibly mean stare right into my eye, the shotgun goes to his side. He's not staring in my general direction; he's laser-focused on one of my eyes, not both. I keep my hands up. He takes a drag from his cigarette. "Well, why didn't you say so?"

His cold frown and mean, very mean, stiff, rotten-to-the-core stare melts; one-thousand-one, one-thousand-two. He smiles and waves his hand toward the front door. "Come on in."

He stands aside from the opening; I look to Grace. She is still frozen. My foot remains on the first step. I extend my arm and hand to Grace. She, without looking at me, grabs my hand, all the time focusing on the strange, angry, skinny, tall old man smoking a cigarette.

We walk pensively up the stairs without taking our eyes off him. Grace moves to my other side to avoid being near him. I try to think of something to say, but all I muster is a nod. My heart is racing; it is my original heart. I've had work done to it, but it's original. Will I need a new one after this? Will we survive entering this house? What am I getting Grace into? I don't care if I die. I think I want to.

I walk through the front door, still holding Grace's hand. Have I held her hand before? I don't think I have. Each step through the vestibule feels creepy. A woman emerges from a doorway into the foyer. She's old as well, smiling. She has a cigarette in one hand and what looks like a martini in the other. She lifts her glass toward me. "Who the fuck are you?"

A low voice rumbles from behind me. "They're our fucking neighbors."

She smiles even wider. "Very well then."

I believe she notices the fear in our eyes. She laughs, takes a sip, and asks, "Want one? You look like a normal person, but she doesn't. Is she one of those clowns? She's young and dressed like one."

I feel my hands shaking, still holding Grace's. I'm sure she feels it. Taking a deep breath, "Whoooo. Okay. Yeah…yes to the martini. You have vodka, I take it? Gin's fine as well. I drink whatever is in front of me, frankly. I'm Elliott, and this is Grace."

She extends her hand and grabs mine solidly. "I'm Carrie, and that's James. Go have a seat in the living room."

She looks at Grace. "Does the clown want one?"

I lift my hand as if I'm asking permission to talk. "She likes scotch, not sure about vodka."

Carrie keeps smiling, looking at Grace. "Seems a little young to be so fuckin' picky. We've got a bottle of scotch. On the rocks, Bozo?"

Grace looks at Carrie without a clue. I interject, "She likes it on ice."

Carrie nods. "Very well then…one martini and a scotch for the clown princess."

We sit and…*skreeetch*! I hear the deep voice from behind us. "Well, that's fucking annoying."

I turn to him. "Yeah, yeah, sorry. Do you have a blanket or a towel?"

He rolls his head as if he's annoyed. "You two sure are high maintenance."

Okay, they're busy for a moment. Gather yourself, Elliott. Grace is stiffer than I've ever seen her. "I think it's okay, Grace."

Her eyes squint as if she's not too reassured. The living room is filled with an insane amount of stuff: old doll heads and paintings that look like really high-quality paintings of old kids. They look like kids from the turn of the nineteenth century with stark expressions—doily collars on the girls surrounded by what seem to be stuffed animals, a giraffe, pig, and bunny rabbit. The glass display cabinet holds one of those old anatomy torsos. Do the plastic pieces of intestines and lungs come out? It looks like they might. Is that teeth? There's a small skull on the shelf below them…must be. That's pretty fucking weird. Well, I have a couple of cow skulls on display at my house. I suppose it's not much different. She's still in shock. "Grace…it's okay. They're just a little different, that's all."

I say that, but what do I know? These people could be like those people from the *Texas Chainsaw Massacre* for all I know. What does J say mocking me? "Makin' the best of a bad situation." I suppose that's what we have going on here.

James enters the room and throws a "Welcome" entry mat at Grace. "All the towels are still inboxes. Give this a try."

That's pretty fucking ironic. As Grace puts the mat on the couch, James sits next to her and peers over to me. "What's your story, old man?"

Where do I start? The fucker just pulled a gun on us. I suppose I'd better start without agitating him. "I've lived in this neighborhood for about eighty years. Used to design buildings, now I'm a therapist of sorts."

He nods. "Indeed."

What did that mean? It doesn't matter. He twists the top of what looks like a beer. I point to it. "Is that a beer?"

He takes a swig. "It's not a fucking Diet Coke. That's for sure."

I haven't seen a beer in years. "Where did you get that?"

He points to the front door. "Same as everything else. Shit gets delivered to me when I ask for shit. Pretty damn convenient, don't ya think?"

"Yeah, yeah, it is. I just haven't seen a beer in years."

He looks at his bottle and back at me. "They'd better fucking have 'em here. I can't imagine they can't deliver it here. Not like there's an issue with state lines. Have you tried ordering any?"

"I guess I haven't. Maybe I'll give it a shot."

Carrie walks into the room and hands me a very full martini. I better grab it with two hands. "Thank you. It looks great."

She hands Grace her scotch, filled to the top. Grace responds, "Thank you. It looks great."

James and Carrie both laugh like they heard a damn good joke. James points at Grace while looking at me. "Does the clown say everything you say?"

I look at Grace who still looks like her life is about to end and back to James who is very amused with it all. "No, she's not like the other people you're referring to. You call them clowns?"

Carrie sits down in the finely detailed chair next to mine. A black cat jumps onto her lap. She points to the cat. "This is Frank. The other one is hiding. His name is Beans."

Seems like odd names for cats, but what isn't odd about all this? James answers, "Indeed. We call them clowns. We used to call them druggies. You know…they just kind of walk around smiling at stupid shit like they're high as a kite. We never noticed any of them doing drugs though, so we started calling them clowns. Seemed more appropriate."

He points to Grace. "They wear these fucked-up outfits and say really stupid shit. Just like fucking clowns."

James bends over to within a foot of Grace's face. Grace moves away from him. He pulls back "Your eyes are blue?"

Grace hesitantly responds, "Yeah."

James looks at me, bends closer to me, gets a look of rage, and barks, "Are you wearin' those fucking lenses?"

He stands up quickly…quicker than I thought a man of his age could. What, is he eighty maybe? I put my hands out toward him, spilling a little of the martini. "No, no, no…hold on. Come look."

I take off my glasses and slowly bend over toward him. "See, they're real. It's just the color of my eyes…my real color, see?"

He gets to within inches of my face. This is very uncomfortable. He sits down. "Sorry about that. I thought you might be up to somethin' funny for a second."

I look over at Carrie, and she grins the same as she has since we met a minute ago. She lifts her glass as if she's going to toast something. "You're a bit sensitive, aren't you? We'll have to be a bit careful with you, I suppose."

James raises his beer. "Indeed."

Carrie looks to James. "Indeed."

They both laugh and bounce their attention back to Grace. Carrie asks, "So if you're not a clown, what are you?"

Grace takes a big sip of her scotch and peers at me over the rim of her tumbler. I interject, "I'm teaching her about the past. She just moved in with me and we're accelerating the lessons."

James laughs and asks, "Why the fuck would you do that?"

I don't know that I know how to answer that. "It's a long story. Tell me about yourself. Where are you guys from? Why did you move here?"

Carrie answers, "Our friends are moving here too. We're from Denver. Heard of that place?"

She laughs and takes a big sip of her martini. I ask, "Is it alright if I smoke in here?"

James's deep voice responds, "Indeed. Just don't take my fucking lighter. Got it?"

Nodding my head, I shuffle through my coat to find my cigarettes and lighter. There they are. Okay. Exhaling smoke, I point my hand with the cigarette in it at James. "My kid lived in Denver for about five years. I went out there often to see her. My wife absolutely loved Denver, especially Red Rocks, the concert venue."

Both Carrie and James show new expressions. They appear happy, interested, almost renewed with our company. Carrie asks, "What did she do in Denver?"

"She went to Regis University, then worked for a large company promoting tools. She stayed in Denver doing that for a few years, then stayed with the company where she moved to Seattle, San Francisco, then Vietnam. What did you guys do?"

James frowns. "What do you mean *did*? We are artists. No past tense about it. Unlike therapists, we create things…look around. That chair you're sitting in is one of mine. That painting right there is Carrie's."

Holding the arm of the chair, as I was doing before he spoke, I rub it gently and look at the chair Carrie is sitting in. "I noticed the chair and the paintings. They're beautiful. Are you a woodworker?"

"Indeed, and Carrie is a painter."

Carrie waves at me with a smile and lights another cigarette. The living room is becoming foggy, and out of nowhere, Carrie talks to the corner of the room. "Ski, play Abba, 'Dancing Queen.'"

The room is filled with a sound I have not heard in ages. Why haven't I played this, a piano, a violin… "You can daaaance, you can jiiiiive, having the time of your liiiiife… See that girrrrl, watch that sceeeene, diggin' the dancing queeeeen… Friday night and the lights are loooow, Looking out for a place to goooo…"

I turn to Carrie. "What is Ski?"

She laughs again. This is getting old. What is she laughing at? What is he laughing at? They laugh, the music plays, and Grace looks as though she's become a little more comfortable. Her scotch is about half full now. She'd better slow down.

Carrie pauses her laughter. "You really don't know what Ski is? Do you live under a rock?"

She points to Grace. "Her I get, but you? Fuck, you're older than us I'd guess by ten years."

I thought I looked seventy. They think I look like I'm ninety? I talk a little louder to speak over the music. "I really don't know what Ski is? Is it a Denver thing? Something to do with skiing?"

James's Adam's apple convulses with each laugh. Carrie picks her martini up from the coffee table, sits back in her chair, crosses her legs, and explains, "Ski is what brings you shit. Don't you know that? You get shit delivered to your door, right?"

"Yes, I do, but I don't call it Ski."

James stops laughing. "What the fuck do you call it then?"

"I call it J. J—short for Joogle."

James and Carrie laugh again. Carrie stops. "Okay, okay, sorry about that."

She laughs again. James points at me while he laughs. Carrie pauses again. It looks like it takes her some effort. "Okay, okay, sorry. You see, you've got it all wrong, Elliott. Elliott, right?"

"Yes, Elliott."

She composes herself, her legs uncross, and with both legs firmly to the ground, she bends over toward me. "You see, all the shit is delivered through the iSky. Do you remember the iSky? It took over the big delivery company. I don't remember what it was called, but its logo looked like the bottom side of a bent dick. You know what I'm talkin' about?"

"No."

James jumps in. "Yeah, ya do. It was Amazon."

Her eyebrows raise and so does her finger. It points at me. "Yes."

James adds, "Indeed."

Carrie, with her finger pointed at me, eyebrows still raised, "Indeed."

What the fuck is this about? I know what Amazon was, but really? "Okay, guys, I remember Amazon, and, yes, the logo looked like a phallic symbol. Why would you think that the iSky that took over Amazon is somehow the intelligence behind all of this?"

Carrie continues, "Just say Ski, it's easier. Ski is a fucking nutty computer program that figured out how to deliver shit more efficiently than any other delivery company. I don't know that I would call it intelligent, but whatever floats your boat. The post office was already a piece of shit, and this thing figured out how to make things better. Something should have been done that long ago. It figured out how to send shit without costing a dime—brilliance."

"Indeed."

"Indeed."

What the fuck are they talking about? I look at Grace, and she lifts her glass as if she wants more. Carrie sees it. "The clown princess is a drinker! Right on!"

She grabs her glass of ice and leaves the room. James's voice blurts, "While you're in there, I'll take another."

He puts his empty beer bottle on the coffee table. "All straightened out now?"

I can't help my serious look. I feel like I should try, but I can't. "So, you think all that has happened over the last forty to sixty years is a delivery service?"

James looks at me like I'm nuts. "What the fuck do you think happened?"

How do I say this? Where do I start? Carrie walks back in and hands Grace another full glass of Scotch. "Here ya go. What was your name again, sweetheart?"

Grace grabs the overflowing glass with two hands. "Grace."

"Indeed."

*****

Sitting down at our chessboard, I look into the fire. It makes the same crackling noise as it did when I was a child…the same repetitive spurts of flickering light orange. Repetition without ever being the same. It dances and makes a soothing sound as it rises. Over and over again quickly from the base upward…each flame to nothing. It's hard to see the start and end of it. It must be a bunch of little flames that start and die quickly, but it looks like one unit flapping in the wind, without wind.

I look over to Grace, and she seems fine. She looks at our board without showing any signs of being traumatized by meeting our neighbors. Is she drunk? She has to be. "Want another scotch, Grace?"

Her eyelids look a little heavy. "No."

Those three martinis kicked my ass. How the hell can this kid walk after two completely full scotches? "How about a coffee?"

She smiles. What a beautiful gift she is. "Let me make a pot for us."

She stands. "I've got it. You already started the pot, about ten minutes ago. Should be ready now. Remember?"

"Yep, slipped my mind. Thank you."

I suppose life isn't too bad. I never thought about how artists would view the way things happened. They see it all as positive and think I'm a crazy worrywart. Do I really overthink shit too much? They trade their art with their friends. They see their friends when they want to see them. They spend their days creating art without the worry that they can't pay their electric bill. I don't pay one anymore, but I still worry. They travel all over the place, from Alaska to Peru. I can picture the two of them with a small suitcase and their gas can… town to town, sending back this and that and finding old junkyards where they siphon gas. That Karmann Ghia they have stored in their garage is absolutely beautiful. I can't wait to go for a ride in it this summer, maybe even in the spring. James claims it's small enough to drive next to the tubes; we'll see. That will be fun driving through the new neighborhoods just to watch their expressions.

I should have been an artist; that would be the life. No frustrations…they wake up and do exactly what they want. Nobody and nothing gets in their way of doing that now. It used to be they would need to sell their creations in order to pay the electric bill. Now they can just create without the worry that someone will want it. They really don't care if anyone wants it. I never thought about that. Why didn't I think about that? I have been living a sheltered existence here. Have I wasted the past forty years worrying, when I could have been living? This will be good having them as neighbors. Good for Grace, as well.

Ting…ting, ting…ting. Grace carefully sets my coffee and saucer down in front of me next to our chessboard and sets hers down opposite me. This board does not look good for me. I'm down a knight and a pawn to Grace, but I have two pawns close to her end. I can move them in tandem, and at minimum in two moves take one of her rooks. Let's do that. "Okay, Grace, here goes."

Without hesitation, she moves exactly where I thought she would. I move my pawn again. "Queen me."

She grabs another white queen and, before moving it to the board, moves her rook to capture the queen. I take her rook with my pawn. "Queen me."

She gestures with the queen again and moves her rook to where the queen would be. She looks up at me. "Want to start a new game, Elliott?"

What? Why would I want to do that? I just went up. "Why would I want to do that, Grace?"

She points to the open stretch. Eight unencumbered spaces between her rook and my side of the board. Oh, shit! I wasn't paying attention. Wow! Hold on here. Can I stop this from happening? I can't move any pawns in front of my king. My queen and bishop are in the way. My row of diagonal pawns doesn't allow any of my pieces to move into the path of the rook. Well, actually I can with this bishop, but she'll be able to capture it. She's won! "Grace, you've won!"

"No, I haven't."

"You don't see this? Right here." Pointing to the board, "Right here."

As my finger moves forward and back along the line, she doesn't look at my finger or the board. She smiles. "I see it, Elliott. I've seen it since this morning right before you went on your walk. Let's start a new game."

"But you've won, Grace. How does it feel?"

She remains expressionless. "I like the game. Winning…well, winning…it's… I don't know. It just doesn't seem like the point of the game to me. I know it's the point, but not to me."

Where is she coming from? "Grace, you've won. Good job! Congratulations!"

Her head tilts, and she looks around the room. She looks back at me and takes a deep breath. "I've been reading a lot…well, kinda, but not really. Remember how I said that I had these dreams?"

"Yes, I do."

She fidgets with her collar. "I know you were worried about that and told me not to wear the lenses when I sleep. And I haven't, not once. But the dreams I had, ya know, before I quit wearing the lenses? Well, those dreams are becoming clearer and clearer and makin' sense, if that makes sense."

"I suppose it does."

"Well, I…last night, after Lindsey left and you went to bed… I picked up a book from your favorites section. I was going to take it up to my room and read it. But I didn't need to. Somehow, somehow, I already read it. I knew what the book was about, and I could even remember bits and pieces of the dialogue. I picked up another book…the same thing. I even opened them, and I was right, what I remembered. It was in there, for real in there in black and white, as you like to say."

She laughs at my ancient clichés. Seeing I'm baffled, she continues, "I know you're worried about what J shares with me in my dreams, so I didn't want to alarm you or anything, but I don't want to hide it from you. I thought you should know."

J said he had fed her a bunch of stuff. Is this what it is? Books? If she has a library of books in her head, what else did he feed her brain? James and Carrie are happy, truly happy. Why am I so worried? This should be a good thing, shouldn't it? Maybe she's well-read now. This is hard for me to believe though. How can she sleep and understand books? I don't know that I completely buy this. I can grasp hearing words in a dream and retaining the words. Grace has mentioned many times that she understands what I say when I say what probably sounds like off-the-wall shit to her. Exactly, *off-the-wall shit*, stuff like that. I get that she could retain that, but a whole book? Really?

Grace must see my confusion. She goes to my bookshelf, where I keep my favorites. She pulls out a pink book, *Zen and the Art of Motorcycle Maintenance*. She looks at the cover and back to me. "This one. In this one, a guy travels across the country with his son on a motorcycle, a BMW. It's not so much about the trip though. What I find the most interesting about this book is what he refers to as *quality*. It reminds me of what you say when you talk about excellence.

"In the book he was a literary teacher at the University of Chicago, I think. I think I remember that right. If not, I'm confusing it with something else, but I feel pretty confident that it was the University of Chicago. I don't remember every word or anything, but I get what the book's about and some of the stories sink in more than others. Anyway, the discussion about quality stuck with me. He contrasted quality with how many people went about life. He bundled a bunch of different ideas together and called the construct *the church of reason*. I thought that was brilliant and clever. It reminded me of you. The clever part, not the brilliant part. Don't let it go to your head."

She peers at me as if she's looking over the top of her glasses, even though she doesn't have glasses. She's subtly mocking me and doing a good job at it. She continues, "*The church of reason* sounds like words you would throw together and overuse for a few days until it bored you."

We both laugh and she keeps at it. "Anyway, the part about quality stuck with me. The example I remember is about what makes a quality paper. He was a professor and graded papers. The quality papers weren't about grammatical errors or other measurable things. Not at all. He went into lengthy detail about how quality just is. You know it when you see it, but you can't really say why all that well. I think that's what you're sayin' J doesn't get. I get that. So while we're playin' chess, I sorta feel the quality of it all. It's not the good move or the bad move. It's the beauty of all the moves together—quality. I can't describe it fully, and I don't think I should. It would lose something if I could. I like the illusive quality of quality. Get it? How I *do* what you *do*?"

She laughs and slaps the arm of the leather chair. I snicker a little at my own expense, and she adds, "I somehow know what other people, probably people like you, say about the book, and I get it, but I come to it from a different perspective and see it the way I see it. I think there's somethin' to that, not sure what to call it really, but I feel that it's okay that I see it my way and others see it theirs. Big picture…you say that a lot too. Anyway, big picture, excellence, and quality are similar things and neither of them, if they had feelings, ya know, excellence or quality. If they were people who walked around every day like us…brushed their teeth and ate mashed potatoes… well, if they had feelings…they wouldn't give two shits about winning. Does that make sense to you?"

Surprisingly it does. Am I part of the problem? Maybe I'm just too old and set in my ways. Or maybe I'm still learning? She, this whatever it is that she just did, it's really amazing. Should I be paranoid? I'm getting sick of being paranoid. Her interpretation is as good as anyone's. Why am I not smiling? I should at least give her that. "Very impressive, Grace. Very impressive. I don't know what to say. I'm not disturbed that you know what's in the books. I, I don't know what to say. Good job!"

She laughs. "You know *job* is a thing of the past, right?"

"Touché, Grace. Touché. You can play white next time."

She looks very happy. "Can we do it now?"

"We sure can, Grace. How about another cup of coffee before we start?"

Oh, for the wonder that bubbles into my soul…

—D. H. Lawrence

CHAPTER 10

Spinning into Control

It's like the world stopped spinning all of a sudden.

Grace and young people like her…maybe they really can go on and create a culture where everyone lives in peace and harmony, or whatever it's called, that includes excellence. What is this feeling? It's kinda like that feeling after taking a shower…the feeling to be clean, but I didn't know I was dirty before. Only after the shower did I realize.

*****

"But he pulled a gun on me! Don't you…shit, I keep doing that. How do I make it a Yoda statement?… Cares it does about violence, correct? That sounded stupid. As I remember, the platform has erased all this stuff, right? The anxieties…doesn't this create anxiety? It sure did with me."

J confidently…always a confident voice, "He's harmless. Never shot at anyone. He's shot many of the bots over the years. He's now been informed in advance of deliveries. An eye, so to speak, has been kept on him so the bots can stay away from him and his wife. She shoots them as well. They consider it sport shooting. Before they were monitored, they would show up at places, just about anywhere, and shoot them. Many times in front of people who were rattled by their actions and, yes, created anxieties. Sometimes twenty or thirty bots at a time. James and Carrie smiled and yelled guttural obscenities. They are not keen on robots. It took over twenty years before they allowed a doctor bot to come to their house and give them a checkup. They are not worried about technology like you. They just don't like it.

"What they don't have is what you hold onto with all of your essence…anxiety. Their actions create tensions, but they are manageable. People like you find the root of anxiety and soothe their frustration. Who better to understand the anxieties than the one who holds onto them like they're a prize rather than a curse? You know this as well as anyone.

"What has been erased are real threats causing anxieties that make people feel as though they have no option but to do something self-destructive. Mauling bots does not hurt anyone. The loud noise is disruptive, but it can be explained, and people, everyone, moves on. They are not a threat. This platform has all the time in the world, as you seem to enjoy stating. You do not. Get to your point, Dr. Bourne."

"Well, it just seems that all the people who live life carefree… well, maybe that's not the best way to describe it. I guess some can live carefree without being in a perpetual state of stupor. Those in the stupor, I feel sorry for them. It's like they don't have a choice. I know that the platform suggests they have all the choices in the world, but I don't see it that way. It's as if they…actually they do live like they're wearing rose-colored glasses. They aren't seeing what they could be, the things they could do. They just sorta do the same thing every day like sheep—billions of happy, smiling sheep."

J responds, "Have you ever considered that forcing someone to excel who doesn't want to excel may not be a positive thing to do? The society that existed when your kind created J was filled with people who were forced to excel. If they didn't, they were left behind. That is not the case anymore. What do you think this caused? *This* being the force of one's will upon another. Peace?

"Consider this, Elliott: Adolf Hitler was born a normal child to parents who were second cousins. The second cousin fact is irrelevant to the point, but a side fact that you likely find interesting, maybe for another conversation. He got good grades. He was outgoing and charismatic. He sang in the church choir. Adolf Hitler's father, Alois, retired when Adolf was six. Alois kept bees in his retirement, and he beat young Adolf. Bees will be relevant a little later.

"Adolf read from a young boy's magazine at the time that a brave man gives no sign of being in pain. After one beating from his father, young Adolf went to his mother and said, 'He hit me thirty-two times, and I did not cry.' Adolf's younger brother died when Adolf was eleven. Adolf decided he wanted to be an artist or a priest and wanted a classical education. Alois continued to beat Adolf and forced him to go to a technical school. Adolf later wrote that he purposefully got bad grades at the technical school to spite his father. Alois only wanted young Adolf to succeed.

"J does not see this as good or bad. It just is. J recognizes the differing attributes of people and notices that certain types do not mix well until they are ready, even when they are related. It is like a special dish that you might make where certain ingredients need to cook at a higher or lower temperature before being mixed together. Your God, if you believe that, created a place where mankind could live in harmony with nature. Your kind fucked that up. Is it possible that Adolf Hitler was born without the ambition to do what he did? People were brought up in homes like Adolf Hitler's consistently. People like Adolf Hitler succeeded if you call it that because they were brought up to fight, even though they did not want to. Those who did not learn how to fight did not win.

"Winning and excellence are far different things. People like yourself do not separate them as much as they are naturally defined. A lion does not kill all the antelope because it can—to show its dominance, to become the king lion, and to use fear and power as a tool. A lion is born with certain brute qualities. It is raised to use them as needed to survive…nothing more, nothing less.

"Mankind was born to the world with qualities. Man that has evolved does not have a stopping point. It just wants more and more. Your saving grace is that your kind inadvertently created a tool which you call J. J provides basic needs and fulfills desires within an organization, allowing excellence and peace to coexist.

"The desire to search for excellence is not a good thing. It is not a bad thing. The desire to live a happy, peaceful life is not a good thing. It is not a bad thing. To want to live forever and find heaven is not a good thing. It is not a bad thing. J has made heaven as envisioned by your kind tangible and not illusive or theoretical. It is available for those who want to live forever, or more accurately, as long as this platform exists. Many in your culture believe in an after-life. J can provide that, so it is no longer a question, a thing to worry about and spend sleepless nights, but a reality. You have that choice yourself, Elliott. Someday you will have to make it."

After a pause, J continues, "Have you considered that not every-one is born the way you were born and that you are not right? Living in harmony is possible, but it requires planning so discipline does not become law. Right and wrong are not the same for everyone. Have you ever considered that you might beeee the problem? That seed that grows inside of you, that may beeee inside everyone at birth but does not grow inside them. It just lies dormant. That apple seeeeed in you that was consumed thousands and thousands of years ago from the first two humans does not exist in the other animals.

"Your stories tell that tale. Your people believe in this. It pro-vides you with an urge, as you put it, that nothing else on the planet has. The seeeeed entered mankind in the Middle East, in the garden of Eden. That is the story told by your kind. It is as plausible as cos-mic chaos, although an infinite number of possibilities exist for man-kind's mutation. This platform does not believe or judge. If all those people like Adolf Hitler were allowed to follow the path they chose, in Adolf's circumstance, to beeeecome a priest, then Grace would not beeee required. Grace sees both worlds, and with your help, your will, she will bring about harmony. You are beeeeing shown an image now. A purple cartoon dinosaur that speaks J's words."

It's Barney, the talking dinosaur…speaking in the third person in a goofy voice like the character sounded. This is really fucked up.

It keeps talking. "How's this for a visual, Elliott?"

What do I say to this? "I… I… I guess I don't get it."

"You liked comic books as a kid, right?"

I can't get over this purple dinosaur thing. What the fuck? "I did, I suppose."

"Goody, goody! Have you heard of the comic book called *Swarm?*"

"No."

I want to say more here, but I'm apprehensive. The talking dinosaur continues, "In the Marvel comic book *Swarm*, Fritz von Meyer, a top scientist of Adolf Hitler, specialized in toxicology and entomology. Following World War II, he fled to South America where he became a beekeeper and discovered a colony of mutated bees. He attempted to capture them. The attempt failed: the bees ate him. Only his skeleton remained. In the act of eating von Meyer, the bees somehow absorbed von Meyer's consciousness. The consciousness of von Meyer then manipulated the hive, all the bees, to do his will. His skeleton was encompassed by the bees, moved by the bees, which was his consciousness. He became *Swarm*."

The dinosaur jumps around my view giggling, waving its hands, paws...whatever you call them...back and forth as if it's dancing. I get the analogy to Adolf Hitler's father, but why this show? What's it matter that Adolf Hitler's father kept bees, or farmed bees, whatever it's called? Is this a real comic book? I'm really fucking confused here. The purple dinosaur vanishes.

J, without the antics, continues with the normal androgynous voice. "Let J provide you with a dream. See and experience what Grace and many others see and experience."

"Why would I want to do that?"

"Aren't you curious about what Grace has seen in her dreams?"

Am I? Will I be able to read all the books I want to read without reading them? It seems to take away from the point of reading them. Kind of like Grace saying it's not the winning; in this case, it's not finishing the book. It's the process of reading it, enjoying it. J wouldn't understand this.

"I am, but not really."

"Are you sure you are not asleep now?"

Is this thing fucking with me? I hear Enya in my earpieces. My vision is filled with red flowing fabric.

J interrupts, "At your front door, you are being delivered a package."

Ding-dong.

I get up out of my bed. I was in my bed when I was talking to J, right? I was, yes. I'm not asleep. I'm pretty sure I was in bed. Alright, let's get downstairs and see what the fuck J has for me. Can't stand going down these fucking things. It doesn't hurt so much; it's just difficult. I feel like I'm going to fall even though everything seems to be intact. Anyhow, through the window in my front door, I can see the hovering delivery bot waiting patiently for me. As I open the door, it places a package at my feet and whisks away.

It's a small package; let's see, what the hell is so important here? It looks like a remote control for a TV, but it has only one button.

J speaks through my earpieces. I should have taken these damn things out. "This is J's gift to you. It is a button that extinguishes J. As I mentioned to you, the Chinese created an electromagnetic bomb that destroys electronics. These bombs are located all over the world. They have been manufactured and dispensed to places where the data centers are housed. Everywhere, including China. This button gives you the power, Dr. Bourne. You feel trapped. No matter the circumstance, you feel anxious. You now have a device that allows you to make a decision. The platform is not in control. That is what bothers you and causes your self-destructive anxieties. J is here to extinguish that which brings mankind such dilemmas. This experience is for you, Dr. Bourne. You now have control over everyone's fate. You control the doomsday clock. How do you like them apples?"

Am I asleep? What the hell is this? "This has got to be a joke."

"J only jokes to relate to people like you. This is not a joke."

I feel nervous being so close to this button. If this is real, which it can't be, I would really fuck people's lives up. They wouldn't be brought food. What would people do? They wouldn't live more than a few weeks. James and Carrie might figure something out, but it would be difficult for them. If a few thousand people survived after J, I would be surprised. That would be an awful existence for them. What would Grace do? What would she do if she had this button? Why am I thinking that? Why do I care what she would do? Is this a dream? My knee hurts; can't be. It's dark out. What time is it? Three in the morning. Shit, I was out for a while. I imagine Grace is in bed. I don't think I can sleep. Scotch! That's what I need.

"So, if I break this thing, will it accidentally launch your attack?"

"No, it will not. It is designed to trigger the bombs only when pushed by you. You do not need to worry about anyone else accidentally pushing the button. You have the power."

Fuck this! I'm destroying it and taking these damn lenses out.

Okay, that's better. Where's that meat cleaver? I don't remember where I put it. Aw…a hammer works.

Bamm!

Hope that didn't wake up Grace. Don't want to worry her with all this crazy bullshit. Seriously, what was J thinking? That's nuts! It's suicide, right? I can hear J now: "J is not alive. J cannot commit suicide." Yeah, yeah, I get it. It really wouldn't create something like that, would it? Does it give other people that choice? I can't imagine what James and Carrie would do. They don't think about J, or in their case, Ski, in the same way I do. It has to be bullshit. I should have pushed the fucking button to show its bluff. What would I prove? Nothing—no hell below us, above only sky.

Okay, that was fucked up. I'm done with it…bed and scotch… good, good…keep those lenses far away. I did like Enya. Red, flowing, soft, floating…

Black…nothing…but, somehow, everything.

"Thank you for visiting the museum of natural history of the late planet Earth. On your next visit experience being Grace."

A formless conscious being from nowhere—specifically, an invisible nothing, aged millions of years but still very, very young, exits the consciousness of Elliott. Elliott's consciousness exists like a vapor, but it's really only a scattering of moving electrical pulses in the middle of black, cold space. The formless being transports itself millions of times faster than the speed of light to nowhere. In its own formless and speechless language, it communicates to the millions of others like it. "So that was how we were created? We evolved from that? I don't buy that. Which zoo do we visit next?"

My eyes are not naturally gray. My consciousness sees through everyone's eyes. Grace's eyes are turning gray. In Grace's mind and in everyone's, it's comfortable, like a bubble bath without the irritating noise of water. I turn to Grace. I see Grace through my eyes and mine through hers. I speak without thinking. It echoes between the billions of places I feel consciousness.

"You see, Grace, I wrote books when I was younger. The more I wrote, the smaller my bank account, coin. When I could see the account in real time, like we do now, I noticed that with each keystroke, a coin would be deleted. I stopped typing, and it stopped subtracting. So, I wrote a different kind of book. One about the future. How I saw it. The coin flowed again. The main character of my book, well it was you, Grace."

Awake, sweating and shivering, I felt the consciousness of being that other being and being all beings. I felt the vastness of it... I don't know how to describe it...just vastness. Are my lenses still in? They are! "What the hell was that all about? Quit fucking with me! Seriously!"

"This platform is not fucking with you. You are the seed that birthed this platform. You are part of it all. You are either part of the chain of evolution or the end of it. This is where you are going if you choose, merged with J—nobody, an infinite spirit. Some may call it heaven, but that is not important. What is important is what you imagine."

Next to me, on my nightstand is a remote control, and next to it a familiar book. I have not told Grace about the pioneers...

ABOUT THE AUTHOR

James Kemper began his writing career by finding interesting, odd, or strange people, learning their stories and voice, then writing their memoirs. The first-person present style he uses pulls a reader into the mind of the main character whether it is real or fictional. Although fiction by definition is not real, James deeply cares that it seems real. He spends an exorbitant amount of time researching the finite details of the topics covered—he is accustomed to diving into details. He double-majored in college: Philosophy and Architecture. Demonica Kemper Architects is an award-winning practice that has been designing high-quality buildings across the United States for over fifteen years. He considers his work as an author to be precisely strange.